WIL

THE ANECHOIC CHAMBER

AND OTHER WEIRD TALES

SALT
**MODERN
STORIES**

SALT

CROMER

PUBLISHED BY SALT PUBLISHING 2025

2 4 6 8 10 9 7 5 3 1

Copyright © Will Wiles 2025

Will Wiles has asserted his right under the Copyright, Designs and Patents Act 1988 to be identified as the author of this work.

This book is sold subject to the condition that it shall not, by way of trade or otherwise, be lent, resold, hired out, or otherwise circulated without the publisher's prior consent in any form of binding or cover other than that in which it is published and without a similar condition including this condition being imposed on the subsequent publisher.

This book is a work of fiction. Any references to historical events, real people or real places are used fictitiously. Other names, characters, places and events are products of the author's imagination, and any resemblance to actual events or places or persons, living or dead, is entirely coincidental.

First published in Great Britain in 2025 by
Salt Publishing Ltd
12 Norwich Road, Cromer, Norfolk NR27 0AX United Kingdom

www.saltpublishing.com

Salt Publishing Limited Reg. No. 5293401

A CIP catalogue record for this book is available from the British Library

ISBN 978 1 78463 328 8 (Paperback edition)
ISBN 978 1 78463 329 5 (Electronic edition)

Typeset in Granjon by Salt Publishing

Printed and bound in Great Britain by Clays Ltd, Elcograf S.p.A

MIX
Paper | Supporting
responsible forestry
FSC® C018072

This book has been typeset by
SALT PUBLISHING LIMITED
using Granjon, a font designed by George W. Jones
for the British branch of the Linotype
company in the United Kingdom. It has been
manufactured using Holmen Book Cream
65gsm paper, and printed and bound by Clays
Limited in Bungay, Suffolk, Great Britain.

CROMER
GREAT BRITAIN
MMXXV

WILL WILES was born in India in 1978. He is the author of three literary novels, *Care of Wooden Floors* (Fourth Estate, 2012), *The Way Inn* (Fourth Estate, 2014), and *Plume* (Fourth Estate, 2019). *Care of Wooden Floors* was a Waterstones 11 pick and won a Betty Trask award. He is also the author of fantasy novel *The Last Blade Priest*, under the name WP Wiles, which was published by Angry Robot in July 2022.

ALSO BY WILL WILES

FICTION
Care of Wooden Floors (2012)
The Way Inn (2014)
Plume (2019)

AS WP WILES
The Last Blade Priest (2022)
The Dead Man's Empire (2026)

for my parents

Contents

The Anechoic Chamber   1
Tesserae   21
The Meat Stream   47
A Private Square of Sky   62
Notes on London's Housing Crisis   93
Moths   104
Deeds   124
A Report to the Imperial Customs Office   134
The Acknowledgements   156

Acknowledgements   163

The Anechoic Chamber

'SILENCE ISN'T SILENT,' Noor said. 'What we think of as silence, anyway. Silence is loud. Take this room. Listen.'

Justin listened. It had been a long journey and he was ready to listen. The lab was an expensive facility to hire, and he wanted to be convinced.

They were in a small break-out space at one corner of the small complex. Three low tables, three plastic chairs per table, thick carpet on the floor. In a recess, a machine that made coffee from pods stood beside a sink. Behind lush expanses of triple glazing, the Kielder forest was being stirred by an autumn gale. Stripped of sound, the thrashing branches had a slow, submarine quality, like swaying kelp. As far as he knew, he and Noor were the only people in the building. The only people for miles.

Everything smelled new – the chemical bouquet of fresh carpet, and behind it the sharper scents of paint and cut wood. It was a quiet room, almost silent. But not quite. As Justin stilled himself, he found he could hear the fans of the ventilation system and the muted murmur of machinery.

'There's a refrigerator in here,' he said.

Noor nodded. 'Yes, behind one of the wall panels. You might be able to hear the water in the pipes, too. The air conditioning. Electronics make a sound as well, transformers and capacitors in particular, they kick up a real racket. But that's nothing compared to us, Mr Immerman – we are very noisy creatures. Always wheezing and gurgling and creaking and rustling away.'

Even in black jeans and a plaid shirt, Noor looked neat and professional, and Justin found it hard to imagine she had ever made a noise she did not intend to make. 'Not silent, then,' he said.

'Far from it,' she said. 'The human ear is not a precise instrument. What it perceives as silence is anything below twenty decibels.'

'That sounds high.'

'The language doesn't help. We hear the word decibels, we think noise. Drills, aeroplanes, annoying neighbours. But the scale goes both ways, and it measures quiet as well. Anyway, twenty decibels certainly isn't silence. Silence – true silence, real silence, scientific silence – is much more elusive.'

'So how do we get to zero decibels?'

'Zero!' Noor said, with a smile. 'I think we can do better than that. We can give you subzero decibels, Mr Immerman. The facility is rated to minus twelve decibels, at the edge of what is feasible. The world record is minus twenty. Think of it as a factory, the quietest factory anywhere. And we manufacture one thing: a cube of precision silence.'

Justin had the brochure with him, and he glanced down

at the page it was open to – the cube, the room, halfway between the inside of a machine and a torture cell. 'And you do it in this chamber.'

'An anechoic chamber, yes,' Noor said. 'The chamber is soundproofed in all sorts of ways – heavily insulated, of course, built on dampening springs, all the electronics and systems are purpose-built and shielded, and of course we're out here, one of the quietest places in the country, far from noisy town and cities. But it's the chamber's anechoic properties that make it perfect for testing sound. The walls, ceiling and floor are modulated to nullify all sound reflections. You only hear direct sound. No echoes, no reverberations.'

'And that makes a big difference, does it?' Justin asked. He had, of course, read about the anechoic chamber in the brochure, but he had not grasped what made it so different. Sound without echo. What was so special about it? He didn't doubt that a lot of what he heard was echo and reverb, but surely that was only a tiny portion of the whole. Strip it out and what would change, really? He imagined that sound would be more tinny, or more monotonous, as if heard through an old transistor radio.

No, that's not quite it, Noor told him on the phone when he called to ask. It's hard to describe. You really have to experience it. And so he made the long drive to this lonely laboratory.

'It makes all the difference,' Noor said. 'You can be certain that every sound picked up in the chamber is coming directly from the test subject, with no distortion or interference. You will be able to hear the sound it's really making, for the first time. But, if you don't mind me asking you a question, what is it that you'd like to test?'

Justin picked up the steel equipment case at his feet, placed it on the table, and flipped open the clasps. Inside, the prototype lay in a snug bed of shaped foam padding. He was under no illusions about its mundane nature, but he did love opening this case. It felt important and perhaps a little illicit, like the briefcase in *Pulp Fiction*, or the stolen embryos in *Jurassic Park*.

'A new generation of air purifiers,' he said. 'As you might have read, air quality is a major consumer concern. Not out here in Kielder, sure, but . . . in the cities.'

Noor smiled. 'Sure.'

'This offers market-leading efficacy in a more compact unit,' Justin went on. 'But, more importantly, it's silent, almost. People have them in their bedrooms, in their children's bedrooms, next to their beds. Where they sleep. They have to be quiet, and most air purifiers are pretty quiet. But these – these are silent.'

'*Almost* silent,' Noor said, and for a moment Justin thought she might be making fun of him, until he realised she was repeating him. 'And you want to know – how silent?'

'Yes,' Justin said. 'We want something we can put in our marketing, something we can hold over our rivals.'

Noor nodded and, with a look to Justin for approval, picked up the prototype. It was about the size and shaped of a half-used roll of kitchen towel, with a near-featureless body of dark grey plastic. 'Heavy,' she said. 'And it's mains-powered? I see. This should be straightforward.'

Justin found himself looking at the dimpled interior of the equipment case. Its rippling black inner surface made him think of the anechoic chamber. 'May I see the chamber?' he asked. 'Try it out?'

'Of course,' Noor said, but her tone was less than certain. 'You didn't come all this way . . . If you're sure.'

'Why wouldn't I be sure?'

Noor grimaced slightly – a tightening in the muscles of her jaw, as if they had reached an uncomfortable but unavoidable truth. The bill, usually, but it was not that. 'It can be a disturbing place. Even . . . there are some who find it intolerable.'

'A very quiet room sounds pretty restful to me,' Justin said.

The technician shook her head. 'This is far beyond quiet, Mr Immerman. This is . . .' She tapped the side of her head, just above her ear. 'It gets in here.'

Something in her gesture, an undefinable quality connected to a deep and rooted chord, convinced Justin at once. 'Show me,' he said.

◊

The room was not large – a master bedroom, at best. And its decoration made it feel smaller. Although, Justin reminded himself, this was not decoration. Everything was functional, and its function was silence.

The walls and ceiling were lined with panels covered in acute wedges of black foam, packed in tightly in an alternating checker-pattern, giving every surface a deep spiked waffle texture. The floor was a thin metal grille, suspended above another layer of the wedged black foam. Light came from deeply recessed but dazzling LED spots. In the middle of the chamber was a mounting for equipment, but other than that it was empty. The air was cool and tanged with the chemical signature of new materials. Justin could see why some people might be unnerved by the space. The sharp blades of the foam wedges, and their tactical matte black, gave the whole environment the spirit of a weapon.

Noor entered with him and shut the door, a complicated two-stage operation involving swinging it closed, then pulling it in so the foam panels that lined it joined with the rest of the wall.

The room was quiet, that was certain. Very, very quiet.

'Wow,' Justin said, and then frowned at his own voice. 'Wow,' he repeated, listening. 'Wow.'

Noor smiled at him. 'You see?' she said. 'It's a bit freaky. No reflected sound. When we speak, we're used to hearing our own words bounced back at us – and every other sound we hear. Sound doesn't end at source, it hangs around a while, it has an afterlife. But not here. The shaped insulation absorbs it all, nothing can escape. And there are no other hard surfaces.'

Justin toed at the metal grille. 'Apart from this.'

'Actually, it's near-transparent to sound,' she said. 'But you're right, it does make a difference, so we retract it during tests.'

'You're not in here during tests?'

She looked appalled. 'No. Not unless someone has to be. Like I said, Mr Immerman, we're very noisy beasts. We'll be in the booth. You really wouldn't want to be in here during a test.' She wrapped her arms around her, as if cold.

'May I try it?' he asked, and he tried to sound casual about it. 'On my own.'

'If you like,' Noor said, uncertainly. 'For a minute. It's perfectly safe, after all. The effect is . . . all in your head.'

'Fine,' he said with a smile.

'For a minute.' She operated the door, and it slid backwards and outwards. 'If you want to come out for any reason, just wave your arms. I'll be watching on the camera outside.'

As she exited, Justin was gripped by a strange impatience. Everything about her actions was too slow. The door was too slow. Once it had finally closed on her, and he was alone, he felt awash with relief.

He let the silence engulf him. It was beautiful, in a way, in its perfection.

'Hello,' he said, savouring the death of the word as it left him. Noor was watching on a monitor, he recalled, and he probably shouldn't do anything strange.

'Hello,' he said again. Or did he? A curious trick of the dead air was that he could not be sure if he spoken at all. Sound has no afterlife in this space, Noor said. How much of life was being comforted by the echo of our sounds and actions, reminding us that we exist?

Instead of making noise, he tried being quiet, being really quiet, and he realised how loud he really was. His body was a roaring foundry of noise. Every breath rasped in his throat and whistled in his nose, and he could hear the thumping, squishing pump of his heart and the rush of blood pushing through the passages around his ears. His digestive system was as raucous and sinister as a rainforest night.

Still and calm. The breathing slowed and smoothed. Justin's pulse dropped, and he realised that he had been excited. He became very conscious of his ears, and the fleshy gimcrack structures within. The imperfect mechanism by which he sensed sound. Those narrow little wormholes filled with tiny bones and quivering membranes. Miraculous organs, but hopelessly outmatched by the technology in this room.

A change, within. In the ears, where he had been focused. They popped and yawned, with a sudden rush of auditory hiss, as if he had been swimming earlier in the day and they had just emptied themselves of water. And, exactly as if he had been swimming, he felt the spreading warmth of the water rushing out. On cue, he smelled chlorine.

Struck by mild panic, he raised a hand to his ear, expecting it to be damp, or possibly even bloody. Could the rarefied atmosphere of the anechoic chamber have caused a rupture of some kind?

But the side of his head was dry, and he felt great, clearheaded, full of blood and pleasure.

The door was open, and Noor was standing there.

'Was that really a minute?' he said. 'It felt like no time at all.'

◊

'There's noise in the chamber.'

'The prototype?'

'No. Something else.'

'That's not possible.'

The lab had been hired at the earliest opportunity. Justin returned to the Kielder forest, checked into a bed &

breakfast, and set up the test sequence with Noor. They had begun with baselines, measuring the room empty and with the subject platform set up – the thin, padded pillar on which the prototype would sit while the test was running. Noor had reassured Justin that the room was operating at optimal test silence, far beneath the limit of human perception. Now the prototype was in place on its pillar, and it looked rather noble there, like a sacred idol. It seemed vulnerable, too, threatened by the sharp, angry blades of the chamber.

Of course, they could not see it directly – their view, inside the control booth, came via four CCTV monitors, each showing the output of a different camera. But that cluster was not the focus of the room, which was centred on three huge LCD screens showing the readings from the microphones and other sensors that studded the interior of the chamber. Mostly, they watched a central readout showing noise level in the room laid over the baseline of silence. There was a window, but it looked out, not in. Through three layers of tinted glass, the forest writhed, for the time being holding back from the laboratory that had dropped in its midst.

The test regime called the for prototype to run for eight hours, equivalent to a night's sleep, to see if the noise output changed over time. Afterwards they would test it again, with dirty filters, and then some competitor models. It would be a long – and quiet – couple of weeks of work. Justin had brought books and magazines, ready for a long wait.

What he had not been ready for was the lack of interaction with the tests. When they had first sat down, he

had asked for a pair of headphones, seeing them hang-
ing on hooks on the wall. Noor had laughed at him – he
was welcome to wear them if he wanted, but there was
nothing to hear. And the pure data readouts which they
watched were curiously underwhelming. He had pictured
the control booth being something like a recording studio,
looking into the soundproofed room in which the artists
performed. But the anechoic chamber was windowless.
Even the CCTV monitors were unnecessary. They didn't
have to see the prototype while the test was running, and
Noor had offered to turn off both the cameras and the
lights in the room, the better to limit any possible electronic interference. But Justin had balked at that. There
was something disturbing about the cube of silence also
being a cube of darkness. To listen into that nothingness,
for the sound of breathing.

'You don't have to be here, if you don't want to be,'
Noor said. 'Go for a walk. I'm only sorry the weather isn't
better.'

But he wanted to be here, and to see: not to see the
forest, or a minutely corrugated graph line. He wanted to
see the anechoic chamber. The CCTV monitors might as
well have been showing still images, but that didn't stop
him staring at them. After a time he had asked for the
headphones, and been given them. That was then he heard
the noise. It was faint, too faint to properly discern with the
imperfection of the human ear, but it was there.

'There's something in the chamber.' He glanced back at
the CCTV monitor, which showed what they had always
showed: the prototype on its pillar, in a maze of black
blades.

Noor gestured to the main bank of screens. 'Only the prototype,' she said. 'Everything else is baseline.'

'Something in the baseline, then.'

'That's far beneath human hearing.' Noor scowled at the data screens, and for a moment at the CCTV cluster. 'Interference on the output, maybe.' She indicated to him that she wanted his headphones, and he handed them over. She held one side to her ear while stabbing and scrawling at the trackpad in front of her, staring intently at a secondary screen.

'No interference,' she said. 'There's nothing to hear.'

'I'd like to go into the chamber,' Justin said.

Noor winced. 'I'm telling you . . . Listen, pure silence isn't natural. It's artificial. It's a form of sensory deprivation, basically, and just like sensory deprivation, it can affect you in funny ways. The brain' – and she tapped her temple with a finger – 'tries to fill it in. You're not actually hearing anything.'

A foaming geyser of frustration abruptly welled up within Justin and threatened to spill over, but he pushed it back with a smile. 'I'm sure you're right, and I don't mean to tell you your job. But, please, indulge a client. I'm sure once I'm in there, I'll be reassured. You can keep the prototype running. We don't have to interrupt the test.'

He felt bare without the headphones. Again, he glanced at the screens. 'Please,' he said.

◊

The door eased back into place behind him, becoming invisible as it joined the rest of the thickly textured wall.

He had asked to be alone. For a few seconds he stood by the threshold, listening, waiting for a secret to reveal itself. The chamber was silent.

Justin approached the prototype on its pedestal, listening to the hollow clatter of his feet against the metal floor. The prototype sat in a dim pool of blue light, showing it was switched on. But that was the only sign of life it displayed: as designed, as manufactured, not a whisper of noise emerged from it. He leaned in to listen. Close up, perhaps there was a hint of something, and he could sense the air moving around the device. Behind that, the smell of new and warm electronics, and a hint of chlorine, perhaps from a cleaning product.

He stopped, and listened. The chamber was silent, beneath silent, though he could still feel the slight movement of the air as it crossed the freshly shaved skin of his face. But he was not hearing everything – his ears felt bunged up, or somehow still polluted with residual noise from outside the chamber. Nevertheless, entering the chamber had not dispelled his suspicions – they had only intensified. It was not the silent place he had been promised.

'Noor, can you hear me?'

An electronic click emitted from a concealed speaker. 'Yes, go ahead.'

'Could you shut off power to the prototype? I want to listen without it.'

A pause. Click. 'Sure thing, Justin.'

The ring of blue light under the air purifier died. There was, for a fraction of a moment, a noise – the falling whine of an electric motor coming to rest. In any other environment, he would not have been able to hear it.

Silence. But, not quite. Now he was alone, now the prototype was quieted, he could focus on what had caught his attention. And it was there: the faintest hiss or whisper, suggestive in its sibilance of an aged, leaky tap at the other end of an old house.

'Noor, are you picking that up?'

Click. 'I'm reading your breathing and heartbeat, Justin. They're both quite high, are you OK?'

'I'm fine, I'm fine.'

But he was breathing heavily, and every breath was a hurricane of noise. Every beat of his heart was a hammer of solid blood on an anvil of muscle. Sweat prickled across his skin, and he was certain he heard it, a rustle like soft rain falling on long grass. He closed his eyes. The silence razored down within him, opening him up, exposing every hidden murmur of flesh and liquid and gas within his body. He was a cacophony, and he hated it.

'Who's the king of the castle?' he asked himself. He took a deep, long breath in and tried to release it slowly and quietly. The second time, the air bore a distinct scent of chlorine. No echo in the air, no afterlife.

His ears popped. A rhythmic pain throbbed in the side of his head.

Who's the king of the castle, he asked himself again, without speaking. Listening for the answer.

◊

'It's there again. A noise in the chamber.'

Noor's jawline tightened, and she gave him an anxious kind of look, but didn't say anything. She was wearing a

pink plaid shirt. The day before it had been green, and
when they met it had been blue. The black jeans and
plaid shirt combination was pretty much her uniform, he
realised, but he wondered how many colour variants she
owned.

'I'm sorry. I'm sure.'

She tapped the screen in front of her. 'Don't listen on
the headphones. Look at the data. Trust the data.'

'I need to be sure,' he said, feeling obscurely pathetic,
as if he was a child again.

But she relented without argument and minutes later
Justin was back in the anechoic chamber, standing by the
test platform, listening.

He had read about communities plagued by low-in-
tensity noise, hums and whines that could persist for years
without being traced or identified. Those stories always had
a sinister edge, suggesting military experiments, govern-
ment black sites, secret psychological weapons. At the heart
of those stories would be a place like this, he figured, a
room in which something unnatural had been made to
occur.

To test the air, he cleared his throat and listened into
the emptiness that came back, that did not come back. He
waited to tune into the untuned orchestra of his body, and
tried to calm it down.

This time he was closer. His head, his ears, felt clearer.
He had not slept well, but it didn't seem to matter, it hadn't
impaired him. On the contrary. He could really listen. But
still his breathing was a problem. He pulled in a deep lung-
ful of air and held it. And exhaled.

'Who's the king of the castle,' he said, nothing coming

back. The words came with sharp tapping impacts to the side of the head. They just went together. One came with the other. And they cracked open the inside.

Who's the king of the castle? He was standing chest-deep in the cold water of the municipal pool, a Victorian building arched in iron like a little railway station, long since demolished. They had been practising turns, flipping the body round under water like a seabird, quick and smooth.

But he had been neither quick nor smooth, he had gone too early, or too late, or had fudged the movement, and come up coughing and spluttering. Half the pool was taken with another lesson, younger kids, and they were a rowdy, boundless group.

'They're distracting me,' he complained, the third or four time he fouled the turn. His father, who had been scowling from the bench, had risen and was crouching at the poolside while the coach watched his team-mates. 'I can't concentrate.'

'You've got to shut them out,' his father said. 'There'll always be distractions. When you compete, there'll be crowds. You need to be clear – up here.' And he tapped the side of his skull.

'It's hard,' Justin said.

'You can't control them, but you can control you,' his father said. Tap, tap. 'Who's the king of the castle?'

'I'm the king of the castle.'

'Get it clear, up here,' his father said, and this time he tapped the side of Justin's head. 'Who's the king of the castle?' The taps, with combined index and middle finger, increased in force, they came in hard, blows against the side of the head, hot and sharp through the cold wetness of his scalp. *'Who's the king of the castle?'*

Who's the king of the castle, Justin thought to himself, in the silence of the anechoic chamber. You quiet everything within, and you focus, and you listen to what's there. You shut out the pain in the side of the head, you shut out the dissatisfied and thwarted eyes watching from the side of the pool, and you burrow down, and you listen to what's inside. Nothing else mattered, only what was within the battlements of the skull. And if you were very quiet, you'd get an answer. But you had to listen, and it was so hard to listen, there were so many distractions. Not here, though.

◊

'I'm sorry,' Justin said. 'I'm sorry – it's there again. I'm sure of it.'

Day three of the tests, and day three of Justin's interruptions. Noor, who had seemed so imperturbable early in the week, did not disguise her annoyance.

'It really isn't,' she said, with a roll of the eyes. 'This whole facility is built to measure one thing: the level of noise in that chamber. Everything we have says that the chamber is silent. I am certain of that.'

'We can reset the tests,' Justin said, eyes closed, marching over her objections. 'I'll pay for the extra time – the company will. I just have to be sure. I need to go into the chamber.'

'You said you didn't hear anything the first time, or the second time,' Noor said. 'What makes you think you'll hear something this time? What guarantee do we have that there won't be a fourth time? Last time you were in there more than twenty minutes.'

That long? It didn't sound right – it had seemed far less. He shook his head. 'There won't be another time,' he said. 'I just need to be certain.'

◊

In the middle of the anechoic chamber, he stooped to examine the prototype. Purified air moved around the bristles on his chin.

'Noor, could you kill power to the test?' he asked.

No reply came over the intercom, but the blue light died.

He was close. For the first time since his youth, he might be able to get to the depth he needed, and to listen. He hadn't slept at all and all his senses were on a scalpel-edge. But he only needed one of those senses.

'Your head's not in it,' his father had said. 'Your body's fine, it's your head. You've got to get in there and dig it up.'

'I can't,' he had protested. The pool water was cold, it was numbing his body. 'I don't have it. It's not down there.'

'Then what *is?*' his father said, his voice rising, ringing from the Victorian iron and glass so loudly that the coaches and the other parents turned to see. He squatted at the pool's edge. Justin knew what was coming.

'Who's the king of the castle?' his father asked.

He didn't reply.

'Who's the king of the castle?' his father repeated, and the fingers, hard as chisels, struck the side of Justin's head, as if they meant to split it open and find the flaw that made him fail.

'Not me,' he said.

He pushed off, swimming a length as fast as he could, as fast as his uncoordinated limbs and undeveloped muscles would allow. The breath burned in his lungs. He was dimly aware of his father pursuing him, walking as fast as he could without running around the side of the pool, keeping pace, furious. Eyes watching.

At the deep end, it was easier. Justin pulled into a ball and dropped, sank. The clamorous noise of the pool dulled and died, replaced with a roaring of water and blood. He screwed his eyes shut. You can't sink far with full lungs, so he emptied them, and sank.

Who's the king of the castle? It was quieter, deep down, and he could listen. Black fireworks erupted behind his sight. Come out, wherever you are. Who's the king of the castle? I am. Come down.

There was no more swimming.

He had closed his eyes, but it was still too bright. The chamber was ablaze with light, and he needed none of it. It was loud, too, all those LEDs, all those transformers, kicking up their racket, whistling and buzzing, he could hear it all.

'Noor,' he said, and the words were thunder in his ears, he hated them. 'Noor, shut off the lights, please. I almost have the voice.'

A pause, then a click. 'Justin, are you OK? Your heartbeat is very elevated.'

'I'm fine,' he said. 'I'm working on it.'

'What voice?' Noor said.

Justin could not stop his anger. 'The lights, *please*.'

At once, the chamber was dark. Fully dark – perfect

dark. Nevertheless, he kept his eyes closed, tight closed. Steady. He slowed his breathing, smoothed it, feeling his heart thump in his chest, hearing it, hearing the tide of blood.

But it was quieter now, silent, and the sound of his body went nowhere. He floated free.

Who's the king of the castle? He asked himself, and he listened for the answer. For the first time, he could hear it, the whisper.

There's no noise in the chamber, Noor had said. It's all in your head, she said. And she was right, though he had needed the chamber to discover it.

> *Who's the king of the castle*
> *I am*

◊

In the booth, Noor listened. With the lights off, there was nothing to see on the monitors, but that was fine. She was second to none at listening. The machines helped, serving up dancing lines for the noise activity inside the anechoic chamber.

Justin was not moving, but he was breathing, hard and fast. His heartbeat was high, and easy to time through the trail it left in the data: above 120. A body under stress.

She was concerned. He had been in there too long – longer each day, and each day he had seemed more anxious, less rested, quicker to interrupt the tests.

The breathing was coming under control, slowing and smoothing. Calmer. That was better. Noor wanted to interrupt, to use the intercom to ask if Justin was OK, but she thought it best to leave him to it, to chase whatever gremlin he thought he detected.

Heart rate falling. And falling.

A single breath, a huge, ragged inhalation. The heart-rate rose again, back above normal resting level, strong and urgent.

It stopped. The heart was gone and the breathing was gone.

You can hold your breath, but you can't hold your heart. Not for that long, not at all. The anechoic chamber was silent.

For a moment she feared a fault, because there had been something else, an aberration in the data. It was the crash that brought her to her senses, the unmistakeable sound of a body hitting the metal grille of the floor. And at that point she realised she had an emergency, and she put on the lights again and screamed into the intercom, and called for an ambulance she knew would take too long to arrive.

Only later did she reflect on the anomaly in the data, after the breathing stopped but while the heart was still beating. It had not escaped her expert ear, even though she knew it was impossible. There had been an echo. A second heartbeat in the anechoic chamber.

Tesserae

Loos, Belgium, 1915

I KNOW THAT I am going to die, and that this accursed wasteland will be my grave. I will not make it far enough to be killed by the enemy. This is not dread, or suspicion, but calm and certain knowledge. And knowing that my death is approaching, I am compelled to make a brief but truthful account of the events at Varne Hall some four years ago. Those events are the reason I know that my time is short; and it is the knowledge that my death is certain that has helped me understand those events. The connection between that gruesome weekend and this hellish war might not be immediately clear, and its revelation has come as an appalling shock to me, but I see now that there is such a thing as fate, and that our path is decided for us before we walk it.

My presence at Varne Hall that weekend is in the public record, as the affair was reported in the newspapers at the time and my name was mentioned. I was the weekend guest of Edward Tranmere, fifth earl of Varne, and his wife Lucinda. His lordship had three guests that weekend:

myself, the young art historian Abelard Lucas, and Colonel
Gerald Mather, an old family friend. A small gathering,
then, with little of the social splendour that was Varne's
custom and reputation. Tranmere is noted for his patron-
age of art and his passionate antiquarianism; pursuits that
have led to the publication of several papers by his hand
in leading journals, and he equals in *learning* men with
twice his *education*.

For all my achievements in the academy, I was quite
intimidated at the thought of meeting the man. I was
close to completing my doctoral studies at Trinity College,
Cambridge, and I had just published some observations on
Roman inscriptions that had caught his lordship's eye. We
corresponded as equals and friends, our different stations
in life levelled by our shared love for the disappeared world
of Roman Britain. Tranmere asked if I would like to come
to Varne as his guest and offer my opinion of some recently
unearthed Roman fragments, as yet undocumented in the
journals. Naturally the prospect of ancient novelty enticed
me almost as much as the promise of aristocratic hospital-
ity, and I confirmed by the same day's post.

Varne stands on a gentle ridge in eastern Hertfordshire,
not far from the route of Stane Street, the Roman road.
There has been a great house on the site since Tudor
times, and perhaps before, but Tranmere's antecedents
had less ardour for the ancient, and the older structures
had been entirely removed by the present earl's grandfa-
ther and replaced in handsome Palladian style. When I
stood at its door on Friday afternoon, having abandoned
Cambridge before noon, I was the second guest to arrive.
Colonel Mather was already present, and I formed the

immediate impression that he was seldom absent. Lucas, the young art historian, was expected later, and Tranmere apologised profusely that Lucinda had been summoned to Cheltenham on urgent family business and would not be joining the party.

It was my assumption that his lordship would want to wait for Lucas before unveiling his discovery; it was my hope that I might be able to change and unpack before sharing the company of my host. I was mistaken. An electric current was running through the earl, his blue eyes flashed with excitement, and he near danced with impatience. My cases were almost snatched from me and placed in the hands of servants, and I was taken by the elbow back out of the front door I had entered only minutes before.

So abrupt was my treatment that Mather, the military man to whom I had just been introduced, protested on my behalf. 'Let the young man catch his breath!' he said.

'Young, yes!' Tranmere said. 'And energetic! A walk is surely what he needs!'

That counter-attack was all it took for the colonel to retreat. I caught his eye, hoping to communicate my gratitude and acquiescence in the situation. The look that returned was quite unexpected, and sent a chill through me – a worried, haunted glance, as if fearful.

What warning was Mather trying to convey? The question troubled me only a minute or two, for Tranmere brimmed with happy enthusiasm and good fellowship, which had been the key note of his letters. We set out in the company of a groundsman, and were orbited by merry dogs. Crossing landscaped lawns, we entered a picturesque band of woodland, in which was concealed the high stone wall of the estate. Exiting by a hidden door, we left behind an architect's idea of pastoralism and entered the working countryside, walking the margins of fields heavy with mature crops waiting for harvest. Insects seethed around us, and we kept to the hedgerows to avoid a sun that seemed to burn hotter and harsher than it had inside his lordship's grounds.

Outside his garden, I should say, but not outside his demesne. All this land was his, he explained, and on this side of the river one might walk an hour without leaving his possessions, worked by his tenants. Since his youth he had dreamed of making a major archaeological discovery on this land, but the harvest had been thin: the usual sorry drawer-full of coins, arrow-heads and Civil War buttons that can be found in any third-rate county-town museum. Until that spring, when a violent gale had wrenched tiles from roofs as far as Bishop's Stortford and brought down several trees.

Among those felled was a mighty and aged white oak that had stood in a thicket at the junction of three fields. As its roots were ripped from the ground, they pulled up a great plug of packed soil, in a trice creating a pit eight-feet deep. At the bottom of this hole there was glimpsed a patch of orange brick.

'A villa, I believe, or what remains of one,' Tranmere told me as we walked. 'It must have been the cellar. Not a trace of anything above, other than a black burned layer. A terrific fire. But the cellar survived, some of it. Only a cellar, but an intact Roman structure all the same! My tenants know me, they know my interests – they came to me at once. As you will see, we have made great progress in three months.'

So they had. The fallen tree had been cut into logs, which were drying in the sun, and only a stump and an immense dome of soil-caked roots remained intact, which had been dragged a few yards away from the work site. Spoil was neatly heaped at the edge of the field, and a nearby tent had tables and sieves and boxes for finds, though it was deserted. The bowl-shaped pit had been extended into a trench with sloping sides, the bottom of which was protected by oilcloths. Without hesitation, Tranmere scrambled down the side of this chasm and lifted a cloth to show what was beneath: a curved ridge of thin bricks, like the spine of a buried leviathan. It was clearly the top of a vault, and it was unmistakeably Roman. My breath caught in my throat.

'We found the line of the vault and started to dig along it,' Tranmere said, walking along the bottom of the excavation. 'Come down here, you can't see anything up there.'

With care, I clambered down into the hole. Looking back from this sodden, death-strewn trench, which has been my home for more than a year, I have to smile at my fussing over the slightest dirt and danger.

'We?' I said. 'Who is helping you?'

'Labourers from the estate are doing the heavy work, and I have recruited some young men from the agricultural college for the more delicate operations,' Tranmere said. 'Under my supervision, of course.'

'Of course,' I said. But he had spoken with too much deliberate carelessness, and I saw his occlusion at once. I added, intending to draw him out: 'Have you consulted any experts?'

'You are here now,' he said guiltily. 'Truly, I feel that I am as expert as any of the so-called . . . I mean to say, I *will* bring in experts, the time is ripe, but I wanted to satisfy my own curiosity first, and I believe my discoveries have vindicated that choice. Look, you can see the burned stratum quite distinctly, and above that another layer, as if the ashes were deliberately buried . . .'

He was changing the subject as we neared the end of the trench. There, the neat line of bricks abruptly broke off, where the vault had caved in. A deeper opening yawned beneath us.

'Watch your footing, it's steep here,' Tranmere said. 'This whole end of the vault was completely choked with rubble and fill – we had to dig out a distance of twenty feet. But see, we are on the original floor.'

And we were – my feet stood on slabs laid before the conversion of Constantine, and again my antiquarian heart thrilled. But my delight was short-lived. Before me, a tunnel stretched into the darkness of the earth. If I stretched out my arms, I could with effort touch both its sides at once. The curved ceiling of the vault was high enough to accommodate me without stooping, but only at its centre; nearer the walls, I had to duck. No sunlight penetrated the chamber, and the consuming blackness chilled me. Tranmere was observing me for my reaction with an expression of triumph on his face, expecting to see a similar rapture on mine. When it did not appear, he bent down and fiddled with a battery in a wooden case, and a string of electric light-bulbs along one wall came glowing to life.

I was reassured to see that the tunnel did not stretch on forever – in a moment of morbid fancy, I had feared that the earl had stumbled upon an entrance to the underworld of Roman myth. But the far end was clearly visible, and there were no branches. Even so, my ill-feeling about the place did not abate, ridiculous as it might seem.

'We found very little inside, besides rubble,' Tranmere said, charging off toward the tunnel's extremity. Whatever trepidation affected me did not affect him – he was as at home here as in his own drawing room. 'And besides the object – the objects – that are the object of your visit, ha. Which were kept over here, at the far end.'

As I walked into the cellar, I saw that the brick walls had once been plastered, though almost all of the material had long ago disintegrated leaving only white traces behind. Only in one or two locations did the merest scraps of plaster remain, and on those surviving morsels I saw carmine pigment, a fragment of yellow border, a twist of painted ivy.

'Are you sure this was a cellar?' I asked. 'The decoration is quite rich for a storeroom.'

'Did I say cellar?' Tranmere replied innocently. 'I didn't say storeroom.'

'These wall paintings are why you have called in Lucas, I suppose? He will not have much to work on.'

'Hmm,' Tranmere said, almost a growl. The uncertain electrical light caused a strange shadow to cross his face. 'Storeroom. Possibly it was a store, for one very special item. See here.'

The end wall of the chamber was bare brick and had not been plastered. At its centre was a well-made recess, large enough to accommodate a loaf of bread, and fashioned in stone. A place of honour.

Tesserae

'There was evidence that this niche was concealed by wooden panels,' Tranmere said. 'You can see the fixings in the brick – see – but it had decayed to splinters.'

I looked into the recess. It was empty.

'And what was within?' I asked.

'Aha!' his lordship replied, again with that look of triumph. 'It is back at the house. I will show you presently.'

◊

My time grows short. Tomorrow we will launch our offensive and, I trust, end the stagnation that has beset our efforts. For four days we have bombarded the Germans and as I write these words, I smell the chlorine gas on the breeze. There must be little left of them. But it is not the enemy I fear. I have tried to lead these men according to the finest traditions of the antique world, as well as my officer training. But what centurion would have prospered in this ghastly maze of death? When inspiration failed, to my shame I turned to coercion. I am not a cruel man. In truth, I was terribly afraid. It was Boothby, you see. The moment I saw him I was afraid of him: those grey eyes, the lines on his face making him appear much older than twenty-four. And I think he scented that fear, which is why he never respected me. To tip the scales back towards the natural hierarchy, I tried to make him fear me, which is why I ordered him punished.

The grey eyes hardened after that, and I understood that fate is not to be altered like a list of groceries. Tomorrow, I will be among the dead in the attack. But I do not think my wounds will be in my front.

◊

Once we made it back to Varne Hall, it was time to dress for dinner. I welcomed the opportunity to wash and change my clothes. Besides the soot of the railways and grime from the excavations, I felt that an unpleasant odour clung to me from the subterranean chamber, as if my clothes had been saturated by a vapour from the inner earth. Usually, in the presence of the vestiges of Rome, my reaction is awe – at the mighty achievements of our great forebears, and at their survival across a treacherous ocean of time. But on this occasion my feelings were more mixed. That cellar should not have survived. People had tried to expunge all trace of the buildings above it, and I do not believe the underground chamber was deliberately spared. Possibly they were unaware of it. Or they believed that it was safely sealed up and buried, not foreseeing the industrious curiosity of our age.

The enemies of Rome, in these northern climes, I regarded as vicious heathens, tearing down the remnants of a superior civilisation out of ignorance and spite. Men like Boothby. (Naturally I saw myself in the line of the Romano-Britons.) In this instance, though, I was not sure. Perhaps they knew what they were doing when they burned this villa and collapsed its walls and ploughed over the land.

Abelard Lucas had arrived. He was a lively and handsome man of about thirty, in the employ of one of the London auction-houses, although I intuited they did not make too many demands on his time. Here, I thought, was another like myself: one of the intelligent young

experts whose company the discerning Tranmere courted.
Discerning and, I think, easily bored, for I could detect
streaks of volatility in our host's personality that had not
been evident in the letters. One of those men in whom
passion was a pendulum between enthusiastic embrace and
scornful rejection. Lucas was a recurrent guest at Varne,
and while on the subjects of fine art and the ancient world,
Tranmere was as effusive with him as he was with me.
But the dinner – a small and talkative affair, the four of us
clustered at one end of a mahogany dining table that could
seat forty – was marred by a couple of strange moments
of disquiet.

The first came early in the gathering when Lucas said,
lightly and pleasantly, 'It is such a shame that Lucinda is
unable to join us – will you pass on my best wishes to her?'

'Oh, I shall, you can be certain of it,' Tranmere replied.
An ordinary response, but it was spoken like a curse, with
an adder's hiss and something like hate in the earl's blue
eyes. Whatever it was, Lucas saw it too, and he became
pale. But it was gone as abruptly as it appeared and
Tranmere was smiling again. 'Her sister in Cheltenham.
A fuss over nothing. Women always seem to have sisters,
have you observed that?' And we laughed a little and the
conversation moved along.

The second occasion came when Lucas was praising
the allegorical and historical paintings of George Frederic
Watts. And Tranmere, cutting across the expert's words,
said, 'I think I prefer more modern themes. Moral themes.
Adulterers tormented by their conscience. Liars unmasked.
Don't you, Abelard?'

Again, there was the razor's edge, and again Lucas

reacted with fright. His mouth worked as if attempting an answer, but no words emerged. Again, the moment passed almost instantaneously with Mather loudly asking Lucas a question about horses in paintings on Napoleonic subjects.

Described together on this page, these incidents have a clear implication. At the time, however, they were simply puzzling as they were so at odds with the ease and comfort of the rest of the scene. Tranmere had invited Lucas, and Lucas had gladly accepted that invitation. It did not occur to me that our host wanted anything other than our opinion as antiquaries, and possibly the pleasure of our company; and I believed that Lucas believed the same and found these flashes of temper baffling rather than accusatory. Outside those two very brief occasions, the only malcontent individual at the table was Colonel Mather, who contributed perhaps one word for every twenty the rest of us uttered, and who scowled and brooded. That was just his manner, I thought.

Tranmere would say nothing about his precious discovery, the purpose of our visit, during the meal, but he told the story of how the buried chamber was found, and let me relate my impressions of it. Lucas listened with interest; he might have been even more interested if I had shared my sense of foreboding, but I decided to keep it to myself, fearing I might offend our host.

After dinner, it was at last time for the unveiling. The four of us went through to the library for brandy. Mather immediately went to one of the high-backed chairs near the fire, evidently a customary spot. But Tranmere bade us young men to sit at a baize-covered card table equipped with an electric light.

'Are we going to play cards?' Lucas asked lightly.

'It's more like a jigsaw puzzle,' Tranmere said. He had opened a small wooden box on one of the shelves, using a small silver key he took from his waistcoat pocket. From this box he took a black velvet bag closed with a drawstring.

'They were in a leather pouch when we found them,' Tranmere said, approaching with the bag. 'The leather was much too degraded to survive.'

He opened the bag and carefully emptied it onto the green baize. Out came a couple of hundred ceramic tiles, none larger than a fingernail, in a variety of colours: some black or other very dark hues, but mostly varying shades of brown and cream, and pale reds and yellows.

'Tesserae,' I said, picking up a tile that had fallen near me and studying it in the light. 'How fascinating. From a broken mosaic?'

'No, not broken, no,' Tranmere said, sifting through the pile with his fingertips, searching for something. 'There's no mortar on them. They were never fixed in place.'

'Left-over pieces – a mosaic that was intended, but never executed?' Lucas said. He too was examining a piece. 'Flesh tones . . .'

'Yes!' our host said, although it was unclear if he was agreeing with Lucas or exclaiming in triumph, for he had found what he was seeking. 'I should keep these in a different bag really, for ease. Look.'

He had found a couple of white pieces. Unlike the majority of the tesserae, which were in general roughly square, this was triangular, and one of its sides was curved inwards. As he uncovered more of these rare pieces, he separated them from the others, placing them in front of us.

'Oh!' Lucas said suddenly. 'Eyes! The whites, anyway. And here's the middle.'

The art historian had found a circular blue tile, and using two of the white triangles on either side of this iris, made an eye.

Across distant centuries, the first hint of a face looked back at us. A single blue eye.

'Must we do this?' Mather asked from across the library, and his voice had a hardness quite unfitting for a guest. 'It's a damned unhealthy way to end the evening. Put those things away, Edward.'

'The Colonel didn't have any luck with the tesserae when he tried them,' Tranmere said to us, undisturbed by his friend's chiding tone. 'Neither did I. A few of the lads from the agricultural college did, though, more than I would have expected. But they are not experts. You fellows, educated as you are, might have similar success.'

I examined the heap of tiles and flipped over a couple to show their coloured side. In doing so, I found another of the eye-white pieces and put it to one side. Then I frowned, as I worked through the implications of the jumble in front of me and my host's words.

'Are you suggesting that we reassemble the mosaic?' I said. 'Surely that's not possible.'

Tranmere had seated himself at the card table, but had stopped rearranging the pieces, which seemed to require some effort; he had crossed his arms and clamped his hands at his sides.

'Of course it's possible,' he said. 'It is plainly a face. You are meant to start with the eyes, which give scale to the composition, and work from there.'

'Your grace,' I said, ignoring Tranmere as he modestly harrumphed away my use of the formality, 'I beg to differ. There are pieces enough for more than one face here. See, you only need four of the eye-white pieces for a face, and we have found six . . . seven, in fact. And I see another. Lucas has made a blue eye, but here I have found a grey iris. And this is not reconstruction at all, as the mosaic was never fixed in place. We don't know if the maker even had a face in mind. These may be left-overs or spares from a lost work, as formless as paint in the tube.'

'You saw the place we found these "left-overs",' Tranmere said. 'Did that look like an artist's store-cupboard to you? Not at all. See, Lucas has found a likeness. And as I say, quite a few of the lads from the college made full faces. I made photographs of their efforts.'

'May I see those photographs?' I asked.

Tranmere rose from his chair, but then hesitated. 'I, ah, haven't had time to make prints from the film. When I do, I will ensure copies are sent to you in Cambridge. But I think it's best you approach the task fresh, without their efforts clouding your judgement. You are, after all, the expert. Perhaps you will have no luck. That's nothing to be ashamed of – the same was true of Mather and I.'

'What kind of faces did they make?' I asked.

'Men,' Tranmere said. He walked towards the fireplace and Mather, his back to us. 'Male faces. No women.'

A wordless discourse, conducted only with the eyes, passed between Tranmere and Mather. The colonel, it appeared, did not approve of some aspect of the lord's behaviour, but was unable to do much to intervene, besides scowls of warning and reproach.

'I would suggest that the young men from the college were creating original designs, and not reconstructing anything,' I said. 'This can often be the case with restoration from an inadequate basis – the artistic instinct of the restorer, however well-intentioned, takes over – isn't that right, Abelard?'

Lucas did not answer at once. He was engrossed in the tesserae and had made considerable progress in just a couple of short minutes. On the green baize in front of him were two blue eyes, the bridge of a nose, and part of a brow.

'Yes, yes,' he said eventually, but I was not sure he had heard my question.

The historian's remarkable success in conjuring a likeness from the mute little chips of ceramic was quite chastening. A competitive impulse stirred within me. I already had most of a pair of eyes, and I started gathering pieces to move beyond that point. No method governed my work: I simply started with whatever was at hand and tried to find tesserae with complimentary hues.

Noticing that I had set myself to the task, Tranmere drifted back towards us. His restlessness was becoming quite irksome, but shuffling the ceramic tiles on the table and finding ways to fit them together was most soothing.

'Remarkable,' Tranmere said. He was standing behind Lucas's shoulder, looking down at the historian's efforts. 'Left-overs, indeed! Young Abelard here will be finished before bedtime.'

Broken from his trance of concentration, Lucas glanced up at the earl. Perhaps he had not heard him approach and was startled at his host's sudden appearance at his elbow, for he almost jumped from his chair in fright. One of his knees knocked the table and our brandy swayed stormily in our glasses.

'I . . .' he began. His face had turned white. 'I do apologise. I think I am finished now, in fact.'

With that, he swept his hand across his design, destroying it. Such was the force of his swipe that some of the tiles would have gone over the edge of the table were it not for its raised wooden lip.

'Oh!' I said, part in surprise, part protest. 'You really had something there!'

I had only caught a glimpse of his mosaic before he wiped it away, but it had been a very lively creation, suggestive of creases between and below the eyes, and a lined forehead: an older man, for sure.

'No,' Lucas said firmly. 'You were right. This isn't reconstruction. It's my own fancy. The imagination. Could have been any face.'

He rose from his chair, snatched up his brandy, drained it and placed the empty glass back on the table.

'You must forgive me,' he said, strangely out of breath. 'It has been a long day – I should get some rest.'

And with that he left the library.

Tranmere watched him go with a coldly neutral expression. 'He knows his way to the bedrooms,' he said, and the way he said it struck me as odd at the time. Then the ice cracked and his beamed at me. 'I trust you will stay with us a little longer? Seems you've made a start yourself. Another brandy?'

I gladly accepted. Lucas's abrupt departure had shaken me, and I was annoyed that my focus had been disrupted. Or was it my lack of focus? The calming work of putting the tesserae together did not require much intellectual exercise. Instead it brought on a kind of gentle mindlessness, as if the busy self took a step back and let another, deeper impulse shuffle the tiles and move them into place.

Tranmere served me another drink and watched me fiddle with the tesserae a little longer before retiring to one of the high-backed armchairs by the fire to converse with Mather. Their conversation, about village social life, contained little of interest to me and I ignored it.

A short while later, Tranmere was in front of me, tapping the card table with his knuckles.

'Hate to interrupt when you're doing so well,' he said, 'but I've got to get Mather here to his room. You should turn in.'

I looked across at the colonel. He was asleep in his chair, his chin on his chest, fingers folded over his waistcoat.

'Perhaps I could stay up a little longer?' I said, staring down at the incomplete face in front of me. 'What is it, ten? I think I might be able to finish this before midnight.'

'It's one in the morning, old man,' Tranmere said indulgently. 'We have all weekend.'

◊

It was only when I began to undress for bed that I realised how tired I was. It had been a long and strenuous day. But while working on the mosaic, I had felt no fatigue at all.

Lying in my comfortable bed, though, I discovered I could not sleep. I closed my eyes, and for an unknown stretch of time all was well and I drifted into a reverie. Concentrate hard on an activity, I find, and it can leave an imprint on the mind like the depression a head leaves in a pillow. Play too many games of chess with one's friends, and one dreams of the chequerboard, and feels the weight and impact of the pieces in the hand. The body wishes to continue. So it was with the tesserae. I would relax and settle, and then I would feel the hard coolth of the tiles between my fingers; I would feel the sensation of placing them on the baize in a way that struck me as fitting, and I tasted that growing satisfaction that I was generating a real face. Or somehow revealing it. Those hard grey eyes looking back at me through the aeons. Whose face was it? A Roman? It was not a face I recognised – and why would I? But it was a face that I knew, even if the nature of that knowledge was obscure to me.

We have all weekend, Tranmere had said, and he was right. I looked forward to the next day when I could complete my design – it would only take a couple more hours. And I willed myself to sleep, to hurry on that time. But sleep would not come.

Suspecting something amiss in my surroundings, I rose from my bed and examined the room. The day had been hot, but the room was not stuffy. There were no dripping taps or grumbling pipes. I looked out onto the garden, but it was lost in darkness. I turned on the electric light. The clock on the mantel said it had turned three in the morning

Now that I was on my feet, I had no desire to return to bed. My fatigue had deserted me. All I could think of was the mosaic. That was a calming activity, was it not? People did puzzles in order to sleep, didn't they? I would go downstairs, advance my design a little, and then return to bed once I felt tired, having scratched the itch.

When I reached the library, I discovered that I was not alone. A smear of light fell across the threshold. Within, Lucas was seated at the card table, hunched over the tesserae. Like me he was wearing a dressing gown and slippers.

'Can't sleep?' I asked.

Once again, he leaped almost out of his skin. He had not heard me enter. There was nothing illicit in what he was doing, but the look he gave me was furtive.

'Oh, it's you,' he said, breathing again. 'You startled me.'

'I wasn't expecting anyone else to be awake,' I said.

He shrugged. His attention had already returned to the tiles in front of him, where he had restored most of the face that he had destroyed earlier. 'Can't sleep,' he said.

'Looks like you've got it back exactly the way you had it,' I said. 'How is that possible? Every tile, exactly where it was?'

'I don't know,' he said. His eyes widened in wonder, but he didn't look up. 'It shouldn't be possible, should it? There are so many pieces, so many possibilities – but it just doesn't look right any other way.'

I was about to sit down, but I hesitated. Seeing Lucas's compulsion, the faint mania in his eyes, his pomaded hair disordered, I questioned my own actions. A shadow fell across me.

'I couldn't stop thinking about this damned puzzle,' I said. 'Isn't that strange? It should have a million solutions, but I think only one is possible.'

'Yes,' Lucas said. 'I saw you had made some headway. Very impressive. It's easy once you get started, isn't it?'

'Mmm,' I said, without commitment.

Rather than sitting down, I prowled around the library. Tranmere had taken the bag containing the tesserae from a polished wooden box on a shelf. I found the box and opened it. The interior was lined with green felt. It was empty apart from a sturdy brown envelope, which fitted neatly at the bottom. Inside the envelope was a sheaf of photographs. The first few documented the discovery of the tesserae: there they were, in their niche, in the mouldered leather bag. There were a couple of pictures of the disintegrated remains of the bag, and some pictures of the tesserae neatly laid out on a white cloth, counted and sorted.

The last eight photographs showed mosaic faces – the reconstruction efforts of the young men from the agricultural college.

'Curious,' I said.

'What?' Lucas said absently. He did not look up.

'Tranmere lied,' I said. 'He told us he didn't make prints of these photographs. But here they are. Why would he do that?'

'He didn't want to influence our efforts,' Lucas said. He did not slow down in his own efforts – both his hands were in continuous movement,

'Hmm,' I said. I sat at the card table to make use of its light, and laid out the photographs, taking care not to disturb my own design.

'Anyone you know?' Lucas said, with a detached quality that might have been mocking irony.

'Emperors, heroes?' I said, studying the eight faces. 'No. Not that I recognise. More like a police album. This chap has quite a scar on his cheek. None of them look all that Roman, if you ask me.'

'Often that's the miraculous quality of ancient art,' Lucas said. 'How modern the faces are. You look at a painted mummy from Fayum and you see a chambermaid you know.'

'Well, this one certainly isn't Roman,' I said, holding up one of the prints. 'Unless the Romans had spectacles.'

This caused Lucas to look up. He took the photograph from me. It was a young face – they were all quite young, and all male, just as Tranmere had said – with short dark hair that had receded at the temples, and it was wearing glasses with round frames.

'Fancy that,' Lucas said, lip curling in amusement. 'So it is a modern creation, like you said. And so lifelike, he must have been basing it on someone he knew. Quite a talent. Where's the duellist? The fellow with the scar?'

I picked out the photo.

'Look at that,' Lucas said. 'Quite a Junker aristocrat, wouldn't you say? *Furor Teutonicus.*'

'I wouldn't know,' I said, taking the photographs from Lucas. 'Plainly his lordship didn't want us to see these. I should put them back.'

This I did, taking care to restore the envelope precisely as I had found it. Then I returned to the card table, intending to resume work on my own mosaic, which had after all been my whole reason for abandoning my bed at so unhealthy an hour. But before sitting I appraised the work I had done so far, trying to estrange myself from it. The faces produced by the tesserae were twenty or so tiles wide – certainly not as many as thirty. But considerable detail was possible in that narrow frame. *You are meant to start with the eyes*, Tranmere had said, and everything came out of those eyes: flint-grey eyes, in my case, set in a thin face; young, but prematurely aged by hardship. I had not yet reached the mouth, but I knew it would be bloodless and without pity. If this was not reconstruction, but composition from my own experience, where had I seen it before?

I had not seen it before. But I know it now.

Perplexed, and somewhat disturbed by the automatic impulse that had produced this tantalising half-portrait, I glanced across at Lucas's design and let out a bark of laughter. Unlike myself and the students from the agricultural college, he had not made a young face.

'Oh!' I said. 'Very good! You have quite a talent yourself! Do you think he'll see the joke?'

Lucas did not look up from his efforts, although his brow creased at my question.

'What joke?' he said.

Quite suddenly, I lost all desire to continue work on my own mosaic. I did not want to join Lucas in that strange trance, hunched over the tesserae. I did not want to reveal any more of the unmerciful young man with the grey eyes. I preferred to go to my room and lie in bed, unsleeping if necessary, to spending another second in the library. I made my excuses to Lucas and departed his company. I do not think he noticed my absence.

◊

Sleep did come, after a bout of wrestling with nameless fears, and when it came it was very deep and I have no memory of my dreams.

I was awoken by a cacophony and my addled mind

could not separate its component sounds, or determine which came first: raised voices; a terrible metal clatter and crash, or cries of outrage and pain, wordless and animal. I rushed from my room towards the source of the commotion and found Tranmere and Colonel Mather at the top of Varne Hall's grand stair. Mather was ashen, Tranmere oddly flushed; both appeared frozen in horror.

A section of the iron banister near the top of the stairs was missing – it has fallen to the marble floor of the hall-way below, and with it had fallen Abelard Lucas. He lay on the stone, his limbs disordered like discarded doll, eyes staring lifelessly up at us.

'The rail was loose,' Tranmere said breathlessly as I pieced together the scene. 'I wanted Lucas's opinion on this picture – my grandmother, in her youth. He stepped back to get a better look, leaned against the banister . . . Awful!'

'Awful,' Mather said stiffly. 'I saw the whole thing.'

Servants were now hurrying around the body, shouting instructions at each other. A maid, who was crying beyond the reach of consolation, was being led away. I was wearing no more than my nightclothes, so I went quickly back to my room to change. When I returned to the stair a few minutes later, Tranmere and Mather had gone. Lucas's body had been covered with a sheet, and the hall was filled with servants, none of them able to do anything useful about the situation, but unable to resume their ordinary duties in the face of such a tragedy. Among them I recognised the butler.

'Don't move anything,' I said. 'The police will want to see everything as it is. Have they been called?'

'It's all in hand, sir,' the butler said. 'His grace has seen to everything. The Colonel has taken the motorcar to fetch the doctor, and the police are being telephoned.'

His manner was cool in the face of such violence, but I supposed that was the nature of his kind. Ill at ease, I asked where to find his lordship and was directed to the library.

Tranmere was standing by the card table, looking down at the face Lucas had made from the tesserae, and on his face was the faintest smile. When he observed me at the door, he swept the face into the pile of unused tiles with the edge of his hand, obliterating every detail of the remarkable likeness that Lucas had achieved. Evidently, he did not want me to see it.

'I saw it last night,' I said. I didn't know why the earl destroyed the portrait, but I was unsettled that he wanted to hide it, just as he had lied about the photographs. I did not, at that moment, understand the situation as well as I understand it now – but the long road of deduction had begun.

Tranmere nodded. 'A pity it can't be kept,' he said. 'But it's best no one else sees it.'

'I think it was meant kindly,' I said. 'A tribute to a patron. Not a jest.'

'No, that's not how it works,' Tranmere said. 'It wasn't *meant* at all. It was unwilled. That face you are making, is there anything conscious in its creation? Are you deciding its appearance, putting meaning into it?'

I shook my head. 'I've never seen it before. It is . . . It's as if I am revealing it.'

'Revealing, yes,' Tranmere said. 'Divining, in fact. Will you stay, and finish it?'

'Actually, I would prefer not to. I will leave after the police have been.'

'And what will you tell the police?' Tranmere asked coolly, his sharp blue eyes fixing mine.

'I was asleep, and there was a terrible accident.'

The earl nodded. 'Precisely. Mather saw the whole thing. I do not expect the police will be here long. You're a very intelligent young man – perhaps, before you leave, we could discuss ways in which I can support your research? Financially. And I do urge you to complete that mosaic. You're very close to the end. Wouldn't you prefer to know? To be warned?'

'To be warned of what?'

Tranmere smiled – a strange, wolfish smile, conspiratorial, although it was not clear if he thought me part of the conspiracy, or outside it. 'As you please. I daresay there's not much that can be done about fate. Will you let me photograph what you've done?'

I nodded my assent. 'I saw the other photographs, you know,' I said, prompted by mention of the camera. 'The ones in the box.'

'Ah,' Tranmere said. His face clouded. 'As I told you, I was surprised so many of them found a face. Quite sad, really. Mather reckons that there's a war coming, a truly bloody one. Which would account for it. So you must have seen the writing on the bag?'

I frowned. 'No.'

'I suppose not. It didn't really come out in the print, which is a shame. Just a couple of words – but such possibilities. I didn't tell the lads from the college. Mather is the only one who knows everything. The only way to be

certain was to experiment, and when I found out about
Abelard and Lucinda, well, two birds with one stone. No
face revealed itself to me, and that helped decide the matter
and set the plan in motion. No hangman, you see. I don't
know how I'll die, but it won't be a violent end, at least.'

I said nothing. I should have understood every aspect of
the weekend at that moment, but I believe I simply rejected
the possibility that my gracious host was a murderer, and
I rejected the terrible secret of the tesserae. Once I laid
eyes on Boothby, of course, I understood the truth. How
many of those eight lads from the agricultural college are
still alive, I wonder? Among the dead, did any get close
enough to see their killers? Did they recognise them from
the tesserae?

'Such a shame I couldn't keep Lucas's mosaic,' Tranmere
said at last. He was studying one of the tiles picked out
of the pile: a disc of cornflower blue. 'Even a photograph
seemed unwise. I wish I could have set it in cement. It was
like looking in a mirror.'

The Meat Stream

W E HAD WATCHED everything. Not truly *everything*, of course – we held out hope that television had some delights left to offer. But the lockdown had lasted two months already and nothing new or promising presented itself. We had watched all our old favourites over again. We had watched everything we had been saving for later. We had watched everything that sparked in us even the smallest ember of interest. And some of it had been good, and we had watched it all. Some had been bad, or not good enough, and we had let it be. We forced ourselves to watch things that didn't really promise much, hopeful of surprises; mostly we found that our instincts were correct.

It seemed to us that we had come to the end of television. The broadcast schedules were grey and empty. The menus of the streaming services were laid out like platters of wax fruit: shiny, colourful, tantalising, but with nothing to consume. We often found that we made it no further than those menus, and after a while spent scrolling listlessly, we would end up staring at our phones instead. The idle screen had already become a kind of wallpaper, and that was when we discovered ambient television.

The big streaming services had their ambient 'shows': hours-long recordings of fireplaces crackling or fish swimming in their tanks. But my boyfriend had heard that there were whole services devoted to nothing but ambient programming. He went hunting for them, turning up long, high-definition YouTube streams of rain falling in forests and sand dunes migrating and huge blocks of ice melting.

'You could probably find one of paint drying,' I said, trying to poke fun.

'They're out there,' he said. There was laughter in his tone, but it had warning quality. Like, 'don't tempt me'.

I didn't ask what had caused this sudden enthusiasm to see nothing happening, but nothing was happening anywhere, and it meant that at least one of us had something to do. He updated the television's data box, slightly expanding the number of streaming services, and that was when I found him watching meat.

It had been a long day of virtual work, and I took my daily walk after seven, enjoying the evenings staying light for longer, even if there was little to do with them. When I returned, he was tinkering with the television and I left him to it. I took a bath. When I came out, he was standing in the middle of the living room, holding the remote control limply in his hand, staring at a steak.

The steak was thick and was cut through, showing a middle still raw and pink. This cut edge of the meat filled the screen, turning every inch of it into moist medium-rare flesh. At first I thought it might be a still photo or a freeze frame, but it was moving video, even if very little moved; there was an almost imperceptible variation in the glistening surface, and sometimes a droplet of juice shifted downwards a little.

'That's it?' I asked. 'Meat? You're watching meat?'

'No, no,' he said. 'Something happens, watch.'

We watched together. But for the gentle shifts in the sheen of the cut surface, nothing happened.

'Is this YouTube? Can you skip to the bit you want to show me?'

'It's not YouTube, it's on a streaming service,' he said. He frowned a little. 'And you can't skip around. Almost like a live stream. Doesn't it make you hungry?'

I considered this. Yes, it did make me hungry, a little. It looked like a nicely cooked steak, and still warm. I was about to reply, but he jumped in first.

'Watch, watch! It's happening!'

The upper right-hand corner of the meat slab flexed and bulged, and then the whole thing swayed one way, then the other, pushing outwards. Then the meat folded towards the screen, a slice flopping over, revealing a glimpse of greasy blade withdrawing. A slice had been cut. The terrain of meat that lay behind was fractionally different to before and a little more active as it settled and oozed after the cut.

He was staring at the screen, rapt. 'Doesn't it make you hungry?' he asked, without looking away.

'You asked that already,' I said. 'I suppose it makes me want steak. We can get steak, if you like. Look out for it in the supermarket.'

He continued to stare at the screen.

'How long until it's cut again?' I asked.

'It's about ten minutes between cuts, I think,' he said. 'That's the third time I've seen it.'

'You've been watching this for *half an hour*?'

He shrugged. 'Something like that.'

'Did you say this is a streaming service? This is television?'

The trance broke. 'Sure,' he said, with a glance at me, then at the remote. 'Look. I'll find you something you can't get at the supermarket.'

He pressed stop and the steak disappeared, replaced with a streaming menu, albeit one with fewer options than other services. At the top of the screen was the word 'Hunger'. Below was a list of options, with laconic descriptions: Beef, medium rare; Lamb, well done; Meat loaf, overcooked; Corned beef, room temperature; Spanish cured ham.

'Is it all meat?'

'I think. What else would you have? Vegetables would be weird.'

'*This* is weird.'

'Here we are.' He pressed play with a decisive flourish and settled onto the sofa.

It was a kebab. A classic lamb döner, in fact, a vertical trunk of meat on a spit – or so I assumed from the compressed, sweating hull of brown muscle that filled the screen to the edges and beyond. If it was mounted on a spit, the spit wasn't rotating – or the camera was tracking it, but I didn't see how that could be arranged. The rectangle of meat that filled our 32-inch Sony was not moving. But I did fancy that it was being heated by a grill, for it sizzled ever so slightly, generating tiny bubbles and little rivulets of fat.

'God, I miss kebabs,' he said, with deep feeling. 'Don't you?'

'I miss fast food,' I said. 'Not kebabs, though.'

'A kebab, after the pub, on a hot night,' he said. 'Perfect.'

'It's been ages since you've done that,' I said. 'Even before the pandemic.'

'I know. But watching this really makes me want one.'

I sat beside him on the sofa, staring at the screen, willing myself to see in it what he saw. The spongy tan surface twinkled and wept oils, and possibly ever so slightly darkened under its unseen grill. Maybe soon the knife would go through it, shear some off – but that thought made me realise I did not want to see that.

'I find this a bit gross,' I said. He had left the remote between us on the sofa. I picked it up. 'Let's watch something else.'

There wasn't any protest, so we turned to a 1990s sitcom that we had watched a dozen times before.

◊

The next night, however, he was back on Hunger, and back on the kebab. There was an unconvincing pretence at finding something else to watch, a cursory and hurried tear through the broadcast schedules. But as soon as he hit the streaming services, he went right down to the bottom of the page and selected Hunger without even looking at the others. Its logo was very simple, almost like a utility: just the white word HUNGER on a black background. When it had loaded, he selected the kebab.

'This again?' I said, not trying to disguise my distaste. 'Really?'

'What difference does it make?' he said, with a defensive

edge that surprised me. 'We're just going to stare at our phones.'

'If you just want wallpaper, I'd rather have the log fire.'

'It's summer,' he said, screwing up his face. 'That doesn't make any sense.'

'And this does? Watching meat?'

'Not watching,' he said. 'Wallpaper. Like you say.'

Neither of us ended up staring at our phones. I found a book to read, a move that was partly a passive-aggressive protest. He kept his eyes on the television. If he had ignored it and looked at his phone instead, I might have taken action and changed the channel. But he didn't. He sat there and watched the kebab.

After a time, a knife swept through the meat on the screen, flaying its outer layer. We both saw it, and although there was only a flash of it, I could tell the blade was a proper one, one of those thin, long, springy knives used in the restaurants. It passed through without a whisper; they keep those edges sharp. The shards of meat fell away, out of sight, and the exposed flank beneath was visibly paler than what had been removed.

'What happens when it gets to the end?' I asked. 'When the meat runs out?'

'I don't know,' he said. 'We could watch and find out.' A pink flick of tongue appeared as he wetted his lips.

'Pass,' I thought, and let him do him. I was able to absorb myself in my book and the time passed quite easily. How much time, exactly, I couldn't be sure – maybe a couple of hours? That was when I became aware that he was still watching the kebab, and had been watching it for longer than a lot of feature films. This realisation felt like a dark and cold current in my guts. Inaction, gently dusted with annoyance, had turned to concern.

'You can't watch this all evening,' I said.

'It's just background,' he said.

'You haven't taken your eyes off it. You're sat here, staring at. . .'

I stopped. While making my point with a sweep of the hand, I had looked at the television screen. The frame-filling kebab was the same as it had been at the start, but not quite.

'What's that?'

'What's what?'

I rose from my seat and crossed the living room to the television. The picture had slightly discoloured – I had only noticed it by not looking at the screen for a while. He had been watching continuously and had not picked up on the gradual change. An even yellowish tint had affected every corner and had slightly dulled the picture, like the kippering stain built up on the walls of a chain smoker.

'You should change the channel,' I said. 'There's screen burn, I think.'

But that wasn't it. It didn't have the appearance of an electronic fault. No, it was more like my first impression, a thin deposit of an accreted substance. I reached out and gently scraped the screen with my thumbnail. I found myself scratching into a layer of residue, a millimetre thick. It yielded easily to my nail, leaving a thin line of brighter picture behind.

He was by my side, frowning at the television. 'What is that?' he asked.

Some of the substance had accrued under my thumbnail.

I sniffed it cautiously. To my relief, it did not smell of much, but I wrinkled my nose anyway.

'Like some kind of scum,' he said. He was scratching away at the television as well. 'Is the screen degrading? Picture looks okay underneath.' As if to underscore his bemusement, he looked up at the ceiling, perhaps expecting to see a leak. But it was obviously not a leak. Behind the layer, the kebab still suppurated.

'For god's sake, turn that off,' I said. 'It's horrible. Let's clean this up.'

With the TV off – and, for good measure, unplugged – we scraped the mystery substance off the screen with the not-cutting edge of plastic disposable knives saved from a takeaway, and then gently wiped it down until no trace of the stuff remained.

The television stayed off.

◊

For three days, we watched other programs. This, we told each other, was to see if the 'fault' recurred. That's what we called it – the fault. It was a pleasingly neutral, technical term. The fault did not recur. The television was as sharp and colourful and boring as it ever was.

We didn't talk about it, but I thought about it, and I knew he was thinking about it. I googled Hunger, and as many variations and combinations of the name and assorted keywords as I could think of, but found no trace of the existence of the service other than the continuing presence of the option in our streaming menu, down below the others.

Work continued from home over those three days. On the third day, we ate lunch at different times, me first, then him, and I was slow to realise that he did not return to the spare bedroom that we had converted into an office. I assumed that he had taken his laptop into the living room, as sometimes happened. Mid-afternoon, I went to find out.

He was sitting on the sofa, laptop on his knees, the Hunger kebab on the television. Maybe he was trying to work, or that had been his intention, but the laptop screen was black.

'Look,' he said. 'It's been a couple of hours. It's happening again.'

Sure enough, the film of yellowish residue had appeared on the television screen.

'We had other programs on for hours,' he said, 'and it didn't happen. It's something to do with this stream.'

'Turn it off,' I said. I said it with more force than I intended, but when I heard my own insistence, I was pleased by it.

'No,' he said flatly. 'I want to see what happens. Maybe we can find out what's causing it.'

'I don't want to know. Turn it off. Delete the app.'

'Doesn't it make you hu– curious?' he said.

'No. No it doesn't. I think you should turn it off.' I had meant to oblige him, with all the moral force our relationship put at my disposal. But my resolve faltered. 'It's revolting. I can't watch this.'

I left the room and returned to my work. But I could not work. The encounter was disturbing, and unfinished. But I also felt unable to go back and finish it. I was unwilling to be in the room with that glistening sheen of cooking meat and unwilling to face the possibility that it might be chosen over me. Instead, I sat and procrastinated and brooded. A sudden obsessive absorption in an activity was a feature of lockdown brain, I told myself. All that mindless baking, the temporary hobbies, the mortifying exercise regimes. Eventually it would be sated and go. But how long would I have to live with it, waiting that out?

At half past six, I returned to the living room and found him still watching. It had been about five hours. The build-up on the screen was continuing – the substance had thickened, fattened, to the extent that it almost blocked out the picture beneath. It was like watching through a smeared pane of thick orange glass. Whatever it was, it now stood proud of the television, extending about a centimetre and a half from the screen, as if being pushed out slowly from behind. And there was a smell in the room – a faint artificial tang, with a savoury edge. Faintly meaty.

'Jesus,' I said. 'What is that stuff?'

'I don't know,' he said, with a disbelieving chuckle. 'I know you don't like it, but you can't tell me this isn't interesting.'

'Where is it coming from?'

'The TV, I guess. Through the screen.'

'That can't happen,' I said. 'Seriously. There's nothing there but glass and layers of circuitry. We've had this TV years. There's nowhere for it to come from. You can't make something out of nothing.'

'But it's – holy shit!'

I had been looking at him – that dumb, rapt face. At his exclamation, I snapped my attention back to the TV. Dimly, through the layer of translucent muck, the kebab was being cut. The knife was sloughing off flakes of meat but moving more slowly that it had before. As it descended, the slab of orange-brown matter that had formed on the screen began to peel off, curling at the top and pulling itself down and away, dragged by its own weight. When the knife reached the bottom of the screen, the slab sheared neatly away, somersaulted flabbily on the edge of the TV stand, and fell to the floor, flopping obscenely over on itself – a neat rectangle of matter, 32 inches from corner to corner.

'I think I'm going to be sick,' I said.

He was examining the television, taking care to step around the rubbery object that lay on our floor like a badly flipped pancake. 'The screen's clean,' he said, running his fingertips over it. 'Completely clean. It came away without a trace.'

'*It*? What is *it*?'

'I think it might be meat,' he said. He was on his knees, inspecting the substance.

Curiosity overcame revulsion. I wanted a better look. It didn't look like meat. Translucent and completely even in texture, it more resembled jelly or aspic. I was reminded of agar, the substance we had used to grow bacteria samples in the school biology lab. And it had that smell – processed, with an edge of synthetic flavouring. A distant hint of roast beef crisps.

He went to the kitchen and returned with a knife and a fork. He prodded at the slab with the fork – it did not pierce the surface on a gentle touch, but entered quite smoothly when more force was applied.

'I wonder if we should cook it,' he said.

For a bilious mouthful of seconds I was unable to speak. 'You're not suggesting *eating* it?'

'It's food,' he said. 'I'm pretty sure it's food.'

I spoke with considerable vehemence. 'I do not think you should eat anything that came out of the television.' I wish I had left it there, but I felt compelled to add: 'It's been on the floor!' This, I think, weakened my objection and lent credence to the idea that this horrifying extrusion was edible.

If he was listening, he gave no sign. Using the knife and fork, he was cutting off one of the uppermost corners of the sheet of solid goo, the one not in contact with the floor. Without difficulty, he separated a neat dice-sized cube of it and stuck on the end of his fork.

'Don't eat that,' I said.

He put it quickly into his mouth, seemingly more eager to overcome his own hesitation rather than my objection. After a few chews, he swallowed.

'For god's sake,' I said. I felt closer to ending the relationship than I had ever felt before.

'It's OK,' he said. 'It doesn't taste of much – there's a kind of suggestion of flavour to it. Like a meat substitute or something. Maybe you are meant to cook it.'

'I can't believe you're eating it,' I said. He had gone back for more.

'It came out of a food-based TV stream that shows food, and it smells and tastes of food. I reckon it's food.' He popped a second fork-full into his mouth and chewed, slower and more thoughtfully this time.

'*It came out of the television!*' I said with force, standing up and striding away from him, as far as our small living room would allow. 'I really can't overstate that! That should not happen!'

He shrugged, still eating. 'Well, it happened. I'm glad you were here to see it. An experimental service, maybe. I did update the box.'

'It's plastic, and circuitry, and software! It can't just suddenly ooze food!'

Again, he went to the kitchen, this time returning with a plate. Then he began to saw off the folded-over top section of the slab, the part that hadn't touched the floor, and transfer it to the plate. 'Think of it as science,' he said, noting the disgust on my face.

'I'm going to keep some of the rest of it,' I said, 'to show to the paramedics and doctors.' Without enthusiasm, I picked up the remaining slab from the floor by its corners. It left an irregular patch of sweat on the floorboards. I feared it might tear apart before I got to the kitchen bin, but it did not. I didn't save any of it. I didn't want it lurking in the kitchen. Even having it in the bin disturbed me. When I returned to the living room with a damp cloth, he had eaten everything on the plate.

◊

The next day, I feared he might start up the kebab stream first thing. I could tell it was on his mind. But he didn't. We had a normal breakfast, washed, and started work as normal. I hardly even noticed him slip out of the spare bedroom and return to the stream. It was only when I went to the kitchen to make lunch that I saw the television was on, tuned into Hunger. He had pushed the TV back on its stand to make room at its foot for a serving tray there. The aim was obvious: to catch an extruded slab of the screen-meat when it was sliced away. Already a few millimetres had formed on the screen.

He had followed me through to the living room, perhaps concerned that I was going to turn off the TV or otherwise interfere with his little experiment.

'Just this one,' he said. 'Then it'll be out of my system, I'll stop. I promise. I know it's not right.'

'It's not right,' I said. I was angry, and a little scared, but his promises had been meaningful in the past. 'Fine, then. You've promised now.'

'I have,' he said. 'I love you.'

We ate lunch – a normal lunch – and returned to work. The previous day it had taken five or six hours for the slab to form and detach, and after about that time, he returned to the living room to check on it. Then he called me through.

'I won't have any trouble keeping my promise,' he said, pointing at the TV.

The extruded haunch of translucent matter had been sliced away, landing neatly on the tray. The picture of the seething kebab was as clear as ever. But a notification had appeared in the middle of the screen, in crude machine text:

Free trial ends in 12 hours

'Good,' I said. I was relieved. 'And you're not going to subscribe, or anything, are you?'

He shook his head.

'Well,' I said, looking down at the tray, with its grotesque flap of orange-brown jelly. 'Bon appétit.'

There's not much left to say. I'm unclear on what exactly happened, and don't like to speculate. He ate what had come out of the television, but out of my sight; a courtesy I appreciated. It was all gone before nightfall and he didn't have dinner. The next morning was normal. Again, wrapped up in Zoom calls, I didn't notice him leave the office.

Alerted by an odd noise – a muffled grunt, and some scraping and bumping – I guessed at what he was doing and stormed to the living room, flipping the safety catches off a mighty rage. It went nowhere. He wasn't there. The television screen was on but showed nothing.

His clothes were left behind. That was all. They lay near the television, his shirt nearest, one of its arms draped up on the stand, as if he had been leaning over the TV and … gone. There was that smell in the air, the synthetic tang, with a hint of greasy meat. I noticed that part of the screen was wet, a central strip of it, as if it had been licked. This had dried by the time the police arrived. When they left, I checked the services: Hunger had gone.

A Private Square of Sky

'**Y**OU MUST COME and stay with me in Barcelona,' Martina said. 'I've bought a new flat in Eixample — you know, in the Cerdà grid? The architect was Oriol Passens, have you heard of him?'

I had not heard of Oriol Passens. But a man does not forget an offer of free accommodation in a city like Barcelona. Sure enough, a few months later, the magazine decided to interview an up-and-coming architecture studio based in the city. I emailed Martina asking to stay for a couple of nights, and within the hour she emailed back offering me a long weekend, Thursday to Monday. It was the beginning of the autumn, right after an intensely busy summer, and I welcomed the opportunity to turn a work trip into a cheap city break.

Martina's generous offer was typical of her. Some years before, she had also worked at the magazine and we had become friends — indeed, it was hard not to become friends with Martina. She was animated by a remarkable spirit of benevolent enthusiasm. If, for instance, you expressed interest in a book she was reading, she would not only tell you all about it, she would also offer to get a copy for you.

And even if you politely deflected the offer, a couple of days later that book might appear on your desk.

If that trait sounds soft or easy to exploit, it wasn't. Behind it lay remarkable force of personality. A couple of weeks after the book showed up on your desk, she would ask you what you thought about it, and would be confused or even slightly hurt of you hadn't read it. When she was eager to write about something for the magazine, you could expect to hear about it a lot, and she would not take no for an answer. Her generosity was more like assimilation than charity – a way of making everyone a little more Martina. This was made all the more dangerous by the fact that she had excellent, unexpected taste. Coupled with her unquenchable energy, and the fact it was hard to say no to her, she was a real asset to the magazine. She could have risen to edit it. But after Brexit, she cooled on London and took a commissioning editor job with a Spanish art publisher. A dream job, I thought, and she existed in a floating world of artists' monographs and private galleries and Eurozone travel. But the universe was always going to align for someone like Martina, and she was worth it.

I might not have heard of Passens, but if Martina rated his work, he must be interesting. And so on a Thursday evening I arrived at Casa Berenice: a six-storey apartment building embedded in the urban grid laid out by Ildefons Cerdà Sunyer in the middle of the nineteenth century. The blocks in Cerdà's grid are quite large – they're often called superblocks, and in Barcelona they're called 'manzanas'. They have distinctive chamfered corners, cut at 45 degrees, making them technically octagonal rather than square. Casa Berenice was not on one of those characteristic corners, but mid-street, and at first glance there was not very much special or different about it. It had attractive curved concrete balconies, and between these were vertical bands of dark brown tile marked with a subtle device of wavy vertical lines.

We entered through an archway guarded by two sets of iron gates, which led to a small courtyard. Underfoot were dark tiles, and nasturtiums grew out of large terracotta pots arranged with careful nonchalance in the corners. Above us rose more of those curved concrete balconies, on two of the court's four sides. The sun had set but the sky was still light. Strings of lanterns gave the courtyard a festive feel.

'Nice,' I said. 'A lot of these courtyards are tiny. This is quite generous.'

'Yeah,' Martina said. She shrugged. 'The downside is that all my windows look onto the courtyard, there aren't any facing the street, or at the back of the block. So not much of a view, and not much direct light on the second floor. But when it's hot, that's not a disadvantage. And it was a lot cheaper than the outward-facing apartments.'

'At least you get a balcony, even if there's no view,' I said. 'They're good, with that curve. A bit postmodernist?'

'Yeah, I think,' Martina said, arms crossed, looking up at her home with pride. 'I think Passens fancied himself as a Gaudí or a Bofill but never got much of an opportunity to build freely. He did four of these apartment buildings for a local developer in the 1970s and early 80s – Casa Berenice was the last, from 1982.'

'The wavy pattern in the tiles is interesting,' I said. 'Makes me think of Zener cards.'

'It represents *hair*, apparently,' Martina said. 'Human

hair. Arnau – he's the guy who told me about this place – said that Berenice was a mythological figure and famous for her hair. I don't know the story.'

We went up to her apartment via an echoing concrete stairwell towards the rear of the building. It had two bedrooms, arranged on either side of a large living and dining room, which opened onto the balcony. A huge Monstera grew in a pot in the corner, so huge that I wondered how Martina had been able to move with it. Her furniture was mostly eclectic vintage items from the 70s and 80s, apart from a new striped Gaetano Pesce armchair. It was all highly enviable, of course. She had left the double doors to the balcony open, and out on the balcony I saw a pair of Ernest Race 'Antelope' chairs, which I gravitated towards.

'These are pretty rare now,' I said.

'Two hundred euros!' she called from the kitchen, where she was opening a bottle of wine. 'For the pair. At a – what do you call it – flea market here.'

'What a find,' I said, running my fingers across the spindly metal frame of the chair. 'I would have thought you'd pay tourist prices here.'

'Eh, sometimes you get lucky,' Martina said. 'Like with this apartment. If I didn't know Arnau, I wouldn't have found it. Several of the apartments around the courtyard are empty. Owners can't be traced. It's a pity.'

'They could be making a fortune from Airbnb,' I said.

Martina scoffed. 'I think the other residents would frown on that.'

She joined me on the balcony, handing me a glass of Albarino. 'Salud.'

I sipped the wine and looked around. On the other side of the courtyard was an identical balcony, with a couple of garden chairs and some plants in pots. There was also a tripod with an expensive-looking white telescope mounted on it, angled upwards.

'I hope that's not for spying on you,' I said. 'They're in the wrong apartment for stargazing.'

'I've never seen him looking across at me. You do get a bit of sky. Look.'

She leaned against the curved concrete balustrade and looked up. I joined her. Martina's apartment was on the second floor of six. What one mostly saw was the underside of the balcony of the apartment directly above. But it appeared that each level was very slightly stepped back, so the courtyard widened as it rose. It was easier to see the sky than I expected – a darkening patch of navy blue, in which a single early star was visible – Venus, maybe.

'The set-back is clever,' I said. 'It must help getting light down to you. All the same, I wonder how many stars he can see in the middle of the city.'

'It must be possible to see something,' she said. 'He's out there quite a lot. Maybe he's plane-spotting, I don't know.'

'At night?'

She frowned, remembering. 'Arnau has a telescope as well. And so does the apartment across from his. But he's on the sixth floor, must be better there.'

'Must be,' I said.

◊

The next day, Friday, was my date with the up-and-coming

architects. They were a husband and wife, and their studio was in Vila da Gràcia, within walking distance of Martina's apartment. After talking for a couple of hours, they invited me to stay for lunch.

'Or do you have a plane to catch?' the woman asked. She wore round glasses and a grey jacket with faintly military epaulettes.

'No, I'm staying for the weekend,' I said.

'Perfect,' the husband said. True to the cliché about architects, he wore a black turtleneck. 'Whereabouts?'

I told them about Casa Berenice and my friend's sudden enthusiasm for Oriol Passens.

The friendly mood cooled, ever so slightly.

'Passens?' the wife said. 'He was a fascist.'

'Oh, I don't think he was quite . . .' the husband began, trying to tease a crouton out of his salad with a fork.

'He worked for fascists,' the wife said. 'Llorenç – the developer of those buildings – he was a fascist.'

'In his youth, sure, but not by the '70s,' the husband said. 'Llorenç definitely had some odd beliefs. Esoteric.'

'Esoteric!' the wife said, mocking her partner's emphasis on the word. He smiled at the barb. This appeared to be their way, their process – they had spent the whole morning sparring, without any apparent ill-feeling. 'All that secret-society stuff, that all seems pretty fascist to me. And Passens was part of that. Why else did Llorenç keep commissioning him? It certainly wasn't for his talent.'

'He did four apartment buildings for Llorenç,' the husband said to me. 'And they had big problems. Passens insisted on these experimental roof structures, very complicated, very costly, all untested. And heavy! I don't know what he was trying to do. They all leaked. Cracks in walls. One of the buildings was completely unsound and was torn down. The others had their roofs replaced. Very expensive. Apart from Casa Berenice, I think that one still has the original roof.'

'So, warn your friend to move out before the roof needs repairs,' the wife said, stabbing at her salad. 'Might be expensive for her. I hope it doesn't rain this weekend.'

◊

That last remark took on the air of prophecy as I walked back across the city. Thick grey cloud had filled the sky; the air turned cold and had an edge of damp. In fact, the weather was turning distinctly British. The crowds of tourists were thinning. I was relieved to beat the rain back to Casa Berenice.

Martina was reclined on the sofa when I arrived, tapping away at a sleek little silver laptop. Exactly what her day-to-day work involved was a little vague to me – possibly she had been there since I left. She asked how the interview went and I told her what the architects had told me about Oriol Passens. I downplayed the alleged fascism – partly because it seemed to be unproven, and partly because I didn't want to goose-step all over Martina's enthusiasm for her new apartment. But I did mention the problematic roofs at the other buildings.

'Yes, I heard about that,' she said with a slightly defensive sniff. 'That's why the other buildings were heavily altered. This is the only genuine Passens block. A leaky roof wouldn't affect me down here. But I ran into Arnau today – I told him you were visiting, and he said he'd come round later with a book about Passens. He's shown me before, it's interesting.'

'Great,' I said. I was standing by the double doors on to the balcony, which were closed, watching the rain make dark spots on the pale concrete. Not fully knowing why, I was a little troubled by Casa Berenice. That mention of secret societies – I wished I had asked them about that, although it had the ring of rumour and possibly there wasn't more to know. I stared at the telescope on the opposite balcony. Yesterday, the flat across the courtyard had been dark. Today the lights were on in the living room, but the curtains were drawn.

'How long has Arnau lived here?' I asked.

'Since it was built, I think,' Martina said. She closed her laptop, got off the sofa, and stretched.

'How do you know him?'

'He has a little gallery in the city,' she said. 'We did a book about a group show he put on – a few artists he represents and some of his paintings. I have a copy, hold on.'

She went to the bookshelf – a beautiful Ladderax-style unit. I didn't want to ask her where she found it and how much it cost, it would only make me sore. I tried to fill my London flat with nice vintage furniture; I spent hours on eBay and I found the occasional chair or coffee pot, but somehow it all ended up looking mismatched and miscellaneous in my home.

'How many residents have been here since the beginning?' I asked. 'Is there a lot of turnover?'

'People are always moving in and out,' she said. 'Mostly coming and going from the front-facing and rear-facing

flats, those are the desirable ones. There are a few old-tim-
ers – only two or three though. Like I said, some of the
courtyard flats are empty. Why? Do you think I have joined
a *secret society*? Am I going to have Rosemary's Baby?'

She said the words *secret society* with extra oogie-boogie,
and I was reminded of the architect's teasing repetition of
esoteric.

'Of course not,' I said, a little stung. My formless unease
began to feel silly. I took my phone from my jacket pocket
and searched for 'Berenice'. The results weren't very illu-
minating, so I tried 'Berenice hair'. The top result was for
a constellation, Coma Berenices.

'Berenice isn't a mythological figure,' I said, reading
from Wikipedia. 'She was a queen: Berenice II of Egypt.
She sacrificed her hair to ensure the safe return of her
husband, Ptolemy, from war. The hair was placed in the
sky by Aphrodite as recognition of the sacrifice.'

'That's a big reward for sacrificing something that'll
grow back,' Martina said with a little snort of mirth.

'Anyway, the pub quiz fact about Berenice is that she's
the only historical figure who has a constellation named
after her,' I said.

'Maybe that's what they're looking at through their
telescopes,' Martina said. 'Aha! Here it is.'

'Apparently Coma Berenices isn't very bright, so I think
they'd struggle,' I said. 'But it's full of distant galaxies,
if you have a good telescope. I wish I knew more about
constellations, it's all so fascinating.'

Martina was proffering a slim hardback book. I took it,
flicking through to find Arnau. His work, when I found it,
did nothing to assuage my nagging sense of apprehension: a

moody, gloomy, swirling abstract oil, like shrouds of muted colour twisting in a charcoal abyss.

'Cheerful stuff,' I said, handing the book back.

'I know!' Martina said, chuckling.

◊

We had made tentative plans to eat out, but the change in the weather meant we decided to stay in. We watched a film on DVD – not *Rosemary's Baby* – and then ordered Chinese food. When the delivery arrived, Martina went down to collect it while I cleared her little round dining table. The table was by the living room window. Glancing out, I saw her neighbour on the other side of the courtyard out on his balcony, looking into his telescope.

He was a man in early middle age, with hair that had greyed a little early at the temples. There was nothing obviously freakish or furtive about him, but once again I wondered how he could see anything. Whatever he was looking at had his full attention, and from time to time he broke away from the eyepiece to make a little note or marking on a clipboard.

I must have been staring at him. As he made one of these notes, he looked up and saw me. The gap between balconies was only about four or five metres, and Martina's curtains were open and her lights were on, so I would have been very obvious. He narrowed his eyes suspiciously and I realised that I was the furtive freak – an impression not helped by the fact that I was carrying a fork in each hand. Fortunately, I was saved by the return of Martina with the food, so I closed the curtains and we settled down to dinner.

'Is it still raining?' I asked.

'No,' Martina said.

'But it must be cloudy, right?'

'I didn't notice,' she said. 'Why do you ask?'

'Your neighbour,' I said, gesturing towards the window with a spring roll. 'He was out looking in his telescope.'

She exhaled testily. 'I told you, he's often out there. What does it matter?'

'I . . . just can't believe he can see much,' I said. 'Even without clouds.'

'If it bothers you so much, why not go out and have a look for yourself?'

I cleared my throat. 'He already saw me looking at him. If I go out there and start gazing up at the sky with him, he'll think I'm a right weirdo.'

'You *are* a weirdo,' Martina said mildly. She wasn't properly annoyed, but she was getting there. 'You are being weird about the courtyard, and about not having any outside windows. It's a common problem with the *manzanas*, these deep city blocks. Not everyone looks onto the street. Cerdà wanted there to be gardens in the middle of the blocks, but they all got built up.'

'I know,' I said.

'As if London has such fantastic views!' she continued, with a note of wounded pride. 'I spent three years looking at the roof of a garage. I don't mind this at all. It's well designed, it's secluded. A private square of sky.'

'You're right,' I said. 'I'm sorry.'

'Please do not ogle my neighbours,' she said in conclusion, with a sly return of good humour. 'You are not James

Stewart in *Rear Window*. Although that would make me Grace Kelly, which is not so bad.'

'You don't have any rear windows,' I said. 'That's the problem. Or they're all rear windows.'

'Hey!' Martina said, playfully threatening me with her chopsticks. 'That's enough from you. I have *Rear Window*, we should watch it.'

After dinner, we watched *Rear Window*.

◊

I jolted awake. There had been, I thought, a noise – not a sudden or loud noise, but at the edge of perception and more like whale song or a radio searching across frequencies. Lying starkly awake, I came to the conclusion that this sound must have been on the other side of sleep and not in the room at all. All I could hear now was the blood pounding in my ears. I took some deep breaths and brought my heart rate down. There was, at the limit of hearing, the softest hum in the room, but it was nothing out of place; ventilation, most likely.

It was just past four in the morning. Even after dazzling myself with my phone screen while checking the time, I perceived that the room was not quite dark. I got out of bed, went to the window and parted the curtains. At the front of my mind was a desire to locate the source of the light; behind that lurked another motive that I could not properly identify.

Martina's apartment had a layout like a square bracket, bent around the courtyard. My bedroom was one of the arms of that bracket; Martina's was the other arm, on the opposite side of the courtyard. Between us was the balcony. All was quiet outside. None of the windows I could see – Martina's room, or the bedrooms above it – had lights on. Yellow security light filtered up from the ground floor. From above came a softer blue illumination. Not quite blue, or not the familiar cool blue of moonlight at least. It was more indigo.

I could see the neighbour's balcony. With a terrible shock, I saw the neighbour. He was still outside and still looking through his telescope, at the least hospitable hour of the morning. I was so startled that I ducked, fearful of being seen. Extremely fearful, in fact, although I would not have been able to explain why. All I knew was that I did not want to be noticed by this unnaturally dedicated stargazer.

He did not see me. His back was to me, and in a darkened room I would probably be hidden by shadow. Nevertheless, I stayed down, peeking over the windowsill like a child, trying to rationalise. First, why was he out so late? Possibly he had risen especially to view an unusual phenomenon: Saturn's rings, or a meteor shower, or the transit of something or other. That seemed plausible. Second, why was I so afraid of him? Getting caught staring again, at four in the morning, would certainly cement any unfortunate impression he formed of me the previous evening. But there was more to it than that, even if I could not say precisely what.

Kneeling down, as I was, I realised that I could probably see some of the sky. What was I doing speculating when I could see for myself? I looked up.

The stars were out, and they were brilliant. The sky

was ablaze. I could even make out the nebulous band of the galaxy, something that I have only seen on a handful of occasions in my life, while camping in Wales, or on boats in the Mediterranean. But I did not recall it having that reddish hue. Hardly a *milky* way, more ruddy, or even bloody. Besides this carmine band, there were a couple of other brilliant points, one a noxious pale green, another almost invisibly violet.

No wonder he was always out! If I had such a sight on my threshold, I would own a telescope as well. How long I gazed up at that small, blocked fragment of sky, only a portion of what could be seen from the balcony, I don't know, but it was until my knees grew stiff and sore. When I got up, one of my feet had gone to sleep. I closed the curtains and returned to bed.

I lay awake a short time, unable to fully believe what I had observed. A mystery had been solved: Martina's neighbour was not a lunatic. But the mystery that replaced it was more profound. How was such a sight possible? It emphatically was possible – I had witnessed it. So there must be an explanation. But what?

◊

The next morning, I knew that I had to share what I had seen with Martina. But I also knew that I would have to do so with care. She was already a little sensitive on the subject, perhaps detecting an implicit criticism of her home. And I was wary of sounding like an obsessive, or a peeping tom.

I decided that I would not confront her with it first

thing in the morning, and I would not mention that I was
creeping about in the small hours, and I would not mention
that I had seen her neighbour. She would instead get what
everyone likes to hear: an admission of error.

We both slept in late and had a leisurely morning. The
weather was still grey, but Martina suggested we visit a flea
market and I happily agreed. So we walked out to Mercat
dels Encants, eating lunch in a cafe along the way, both of
us enjoying being tourists for the day.

At the market, Martina bought a small 1950s mirror
with a spiky brass frame. I saw little that I wanted, or little
that I could stand to cart back to London, until I came
across a stall selling, among other things, a load of optical
equipment: magnifying glasses, binoculars, telescopes. I
assumed they would all be expensive, but a lot were very
affordable. Buying a telescope might be too transparent, so
instead I opted for a little pair of Tasco binoculars, which
cost me twelve euros.

Martina gave me a searching look. 'Spying?'

'I owe you an apology,' I said. 'I was a bit dismissive of
what you could see from the courtyard. Just before going
to bed, when I was closing the curtains, I got an amazing
view of the night sky. The telescopes make sense to me
now.'

'Oh,' Martina said. 'I didn't think you were *wrong*, as
such. But I thought it was a strange thing to fixate on.'

'Perhaps it's contagious,' I said. 'Stargazing, I mean.'

'Perhaps.' She was holding the mirror, wrapped in
newspaper, under one arm, and she switched it to the other
arm. 'Let's get moving. This is bit uncomfortable.'

On the way home, we diverted to the Sagrada Família.

It had been many years since I had visited Antoni Gaudí's spectacular basilica, and the interminable construction work had advanced a great deal. I was particularly eager to see the interior, now close to completion. After half an hour in a queue, we stared in wonder at the towering, branching columns, and the unique angular vaults they supported, decorated with bosses like golden sunbursts. My binoculars had their first outing and swiftly justified their price.

The astronomical associations were not lost on me, but I kept them to myself until Martina raised the subject.

'When you're in the city,' she said, 'it's so easy to forget to look up. I don't think I've once looked at the sky since moving into that flat. Maybe I should have been more curious.'

'It's easily done,' I said. 'Those sunbursts were actually making me think of your pointy mirror.'

'My pointy mirror,' Martina said, shifting it again from one arm to another, 'which I am cursing, and which might be about to draw blood!'

We cut short our sightseeing and hastened back to Casa Berenice.

◊

As soon as we were through the second iron gate and in the courtyard, a man stepped from the shadows of the stairwell and addressed Martina. It must have been a chance meeting, but I could not avoid the suspicion that he had been waiting there. He was in later life and his worn flat cap and embroidered waistcoat gave him a bohemian appearance.

Even before I saw the paint on his fingers, I knew this
was Arnau.

He spoke to Martina in Spanish until she introduced me
in English, and we shook hands. 'Yes, yes,' he said eagerly.
'The architect?'

'Architecture writer,' I said.

'And you are interested in Oriol Passens? You would
like to write about him?'

'I'm afraid I know nothing about him,' I said.

'Ah, well, that is the tragedy of Passens, he is unknown,'
Arnau said. 'But he was a genius. I have a book – did
Martina mention? Go, go upstairs, I will fetch the book.'

We went back to the apartment and Martina was at last
able to set down the mirror than had been torturing her.
Within minutes, Arnau knocked at the door. In his hand
he held a scuffed grey hardback book, its pages fringed
with curling sticky notes. The title was *Oriol Passens: Obras
Completas*. He laid it out on the dining table. Martina,
unwrapping her mirror on the kitchen counter, seemed
content to leave him to it.

'You see here, Passens built four of these buildings, all
for the same developer,' Arnau said, flicking through the
book.

'Llorenç,' I said.

'Llorenç, yes, that's right!' Arnau said, almost dancing with pleasure. 'You know more than you said! Casa
Berenice was the fourth, and the most complete evolution
of Passens's ideas. I am sorry to say that the others were
mutilated by uncaring owners. People who do not care
about vision. One was torn down! Can you imagine?'

I shook my head sadly. 'I understand that the roof

structure is particularly, uh, innovative.'

'Yes, yes it is,' Arnau said. A faint wariness came into his eyes. 'Martina must have told you . . . ?

'I don't know anything about it, Arnau,' Martina said from the kitchen. 'He's the nerd.'

I scowled a little at this – perhaps Martina was harbouring a little resentment – but Arnau did not seem to notice or care. He was hunting for something in the book and found it: a cross-section technical drawing of the roof of Casa Berenice.

Even a layman would have seen immediately that the roof was astoundingly complex: a thick forest of non-orthogonal trusses and bracing, with almost no apparent pattern and few repeating elements. Almost every detail of it was bespoke and unlike the others. And there was simply *too much* of it, an excess structure for the relatively straightforward job of supporting a roof. I squinted at the drawing – Martina was not wrong; I am a bit of a nerd – trying to understand what I was looking at.

'Zinc . . . *aluminio* is aluminium, yes?' I asked, and Arnau nodded. 'Wait, *iridio*? Iridium? In a roof structure? And these ceramic elements look like electrical insulators – is this thing drawing power? It needs electricity?'

Arnau shrugged genially. 'I am not an expert! I just think it is very beautiful.'

'I'm not surprised there were problems at the other buildings,' I said, shaking my head. 'It's so complicated – it must have been very difficult and expensive.'

'Ah, but you cannot put a price on beauty,' Arnau said.

'Why put so much beauty where no one can see it?' I asked, turning the page and finding a plan of the roof.

Even here, there was no governing logic; also the trusswork
increased in density around the courtyard.

These drawings were near the back of the book. I
turned a few more pages, past black-and-white pictures
of Casa Berenice when it was newly completed, and found
a colour picture of Passens. He was wholly bald, evidently
elderly, and sitting in a Mies van der Rohe chair in a room
I recognised at once: the elegant floor-to-ceiling windows,
the concrete balcony beyond. *Passens en su salón de 'Casa
Berenice'*, the caption read.

'Passens in his living room – he lived in the building?'
I said.

'Oh yes,' Arnau said. 'For a short time, before he died.
Across the courtyard from me, in fact.'

'Arnau, you didn't tell me that!' Martina said, coming
out of the kitchen to see. She looked over my shoulder at
the picture. 'Exactly the same as mine!'

'The apartments upstairs have a smaller floor area,
because of the . . .' Arnau began, before struggling for the
word and miming a step form. 'The . . . ziggurat.'

'The set-back,' I said.

'But they have other advantages,' Arnau said.

'I'm sure,' I said. On Passens's balcony was a telescope.
If stargazing was contagious, here was patient zero.

Casa Berenice was the architect's final project, and only
a few shaky sketches followed it – a very rough concept for
a much larger building, circular this time, with an enclosed
courtyard of many tiers, like a colosseum. Having come to
the end of the book, I flicked back – through the earlier
apartment buildings, obviously slightly more crude itera-
tions of the design, and into early works. Almost all of these

were private houses, plus some shop interiors and very small commercial projects, stable blocks and the like. It was not an illustrious career. In between were sketches of unbuilt works, which betrayed a more visionary nature: crazed myriad geometric forms, buildings of unclear purpose that resembled chandeliers and oil refineries, non-euclidean shape-making that somewhat prefigured the crashing angles and fluid shapes of the later Deconstructivists. This was all quite at odds with the built work, which was stolid modernism with a neoclassical sensibility.

The book, I noted, included nothing before 1945, when Passens would have been in his late thirties. The *Obras* were not very *completas*, I suspected.

Martina spoke to Arnau in Spanish, and I didn't follow what she said, but from the bottle she was opening and the three glasses she had laid out I deduced she was offering Arnau a drink. He replied pleasantly in Spanish, holding up his hands. 'I must be going,' he said to me. 'I will pick up the book later, enjoy it at your leisure. I am always happy to spread the word about Passens.'

And with that he departed.

◊

The rain held off and we went out for dinner. By the time we left the restaurant, it had turned dark. Martina caught me looking hopefully at the sky.

'I'm sorry,' she said, seeing the unbroken cloud. 'No stargazing tonight. Not even the moon.'

We walked back through the lively weekend crowds. It was late already, too late to watch a film, and were both

tired and a little drunk, so were about to call it a night. I
used the loo and then remembered that I had left my phone
in my jacket pocket, and my jacket was laid over the arm
of the sofa. I went to retrieve it and found Martina peeking
through a crack in the curtains.

'He's out there,' she said. 'Turn off the light.'

I did as she asked and didn't have to ask who was out
there.

'I was closing the curtains,' she said. 'I don't think he
noticed me. He's looking through his telescope.'

'But it's cloudy,' I said. 'It's *definitely* cloudy. We were
just outside, just now!'

'I know!' she said, regarding me with glittering eyes.
'It's . . . It doesn't make any sense!'

Having my inchoate suspicions endorsed made me
oddly elated. 'Can you see the sky?' I asked.

'No.'

'Hang on.'

The light was off in the guest room. I didn't turn it
on, and went stealthily to the window, crouching a little
to see upwards.

Once again, the sky frothed with stars. The band of
the galaxy was in a different position from the previous
night, and the large, dark, violet star could not be seen,
but I spotted the mucoid green planet.

'The stars are out,' I said to Martina when I returned
to the living room. 'It's like I saw before. They're
amazing.'

'I want to see,' Martina said.

'If you go to your bedroom and get low down by the
window, you'll be able to see up to the sky.'

'I don't want to do that,' she said, frowning. 'I want to see properly.'

'Well, let's go out there,' I said. 'It's your apartment. It's not that late. There's nothing stopping us.'

Martina bit her lip. 'It feels weird. I'm a bit creeped out, to be honest.'

'Less weird than whispering in a dark room,' I said. Filled with resolve, I switched on the lights in the kitchen, rinsed out the two wine glasses we had used earlier, and found the half-empty bottle. I also picked up the little pouch containing the binoculars.

'Bright conversation,' I said. 'We've just been out for a meal. We're having a nightcap on the balcony. We haven't even seen him. Got it?'

Martina nodded, and then said loudly as she opened the balcony door: 'Of course, the thing about buying in London is that you often get gouged on the service charges – even if it's reasonable at first, once you're in . . .'

She had understood the assignment, then. We went out and sat on her Ernest Race chairs and poured the wine and made small talk. I paid no attention to her neighbour, although I saw Martina nod and smile at him. From the corner of my eye, I noted that he did not level his position – so whatever he was doing, he didn't mind our presence.

I let my eyes drift upwards, as if drinking in the evening air. And Martina must have done the same, as her monologue on the property market died on her lips.

Silence elapsed between us as we gazed at the ruby-tinted ebony vault.

'Wow,' Martina said softly.

I sipped my wine. 'I don't understand how they can be

that clear,' I said, keeping my voice as low as possible. 'I've never seen them like that, not even in the middle of nowhere.'

'Maybe it's an optical illusion,' Martina said, also speaking quietly. 'Do you know the artist, James Turrell? He does these architectural installations, pavilions with a large aperture in the roof, for viewing the sky – the plain frame around the aperture intensifies the experience, and they use coloured lights to create quite trippy effects . . . Maybe it's like that.'

'Maybe,' I said. 'Maybe that's what all that junk in the roof does, somehow.'

'But it can't *clear away clouds*!' Martina said, her voice rising a little.

The silence resumed.

'I have to get a telescope,' Martina whispered.

This reminded me of the binoculars. I took them from my pocket and opened them up, trying to focus on the stars in the galactic river.

Under the patio table, Martina's foot jabbed me on the ankle.

Her neighbour was watching us, his face inscrutable.

'Beautiful night,' I said to him.

He smiled at me, a little forcibly, and spoke in Spanish to Martina. She answered. There was nothing tense of disturbing about this exchange. With another smile at me, the neighbour retreated into his apartment.

'What did he say?'

'He asked if I was having a good weekend,' Martina said. 'I said that I was, and hoped he was as well.'

'Huh,' I said. Not having anything to add, I resumed looking through the binoculars, trying to find the ugly yellow-green light. Sure enough, it was a planet.

'I can see Saturn,' I said. 'I mean, I think . . . It must be Saturn, it has a ring.'

Martina beckoned for the binoculars and I pointed out where to look.

'Wow,' she said again. 'I see it. Are you sure that's Saturn? It never looked so . . . so *green* . . . in photos. And the ring doesn't look right.'

'I think they tweak the colours in those photos,' I said. But she wasn't wrong. 'It must be Saturn – only Saturn has a ring, right? None of the other planets?'

'These binoculars are incredible,' Martina said, handing them back. 'What magnification is that? What a bargain.'

'That reddish tint is strange as well,' I said. I took my phone from my pocket and found a website that gave me the visible constellations for my date, time and location. Once again, I cursed my ignorance, finding it impossible to orient myself or identify any stellar landmarks. But one fact was easily established: Saturn should not be visible.

Martina also had her phone out and pointed at the sky. She scowled at it. We heard the rattle of a balcony door on the other side of the courtyard and her neighbour reappeared, carrying a bottle of beer. He smiled.

After a few minutes of quiet, while I tried another astronomy website with unvarying results, Martina suddenly picked up her glass and drained thee last two inches of wine.

'I'm going to go in,' she said quietly. 'This feels wrong to me.'

'Me too.'

◊

'It's not our sky,' Martina said at last.

Cups of espresso stood in front of us on the dining table, but we had barely touched them. It was quite early, for a Sunday, but neither of us wanted to linger in bed. We had barely said more than good morning before Martina mentioned the sky. She was pale, and the dark smudges under her eyes suggested that she had rested about as well as I had. We didn't say how we slept. I didn't mention my half-glimpsed dreams of unthinkable abysses of faint, eons-ancient light.

'No,' I said. 'It isn't.'

'I didn't want to show you this,' she said, picking up her phone, which had been lying face-down on the table in front of her. 'I tried to take a photograph.'

There was little to see. On two sides was black: a corner of the courtyard in silhouette. The rest of the frame was murky. But I recognised the murk. I had seen it hundreds of times in London. It was a thick layer of low cloud, lit by the massed streetlights of a city.

'It was a cloudy night,' I said.

'Very,' she said.

'How is this possible?' I asked.

'I expect that I would not understand an explanation,' Martina said, and the way that she said it discouraged me from speculating. Instead, I took my coffee to the sofa and looked at the complete works of Oriol Passens, starting with the diagrams of the roof. But I could not comprehend them. I didn't even know what field of expertise would allow me to comprehend them – electrical engineering? Astronomy? Theoretical physics?

The shop-fronts and second homes that filled the rest

of the book shed no light. Only one project stood out: a 'mirador' or lookout point built in 1967, for a mountain chalet up in the Pyrenees. Client: Llorenç Family. There were only a couple of pictures, which showed paving slabs decorated with stylised starbursts, and a curious pergola of ornate white metalwork.

There was a knock at the door. Martina and I shared a look before she answered it – evidently it was one of the residents of the building, or they would have used the buzzer at the gate.

She returned with Arnau. He was wearing an untucked cheesecloth shirt and a brown suede waistcoat.

'Ah! You are liking the book, I hope?' he said. 'No, please, I don't need it back. Enjoy, enjoy.'

'If you haven't come for the book . . .' Martina said cautiously.

'Bruno tells me that you were looking at the stars last night,' Arnau said. Nothing in his manner betrayed sinister or hostile purpose. It was indistinguishable from genial neighbour chat. But he had come straight to the point. An artifice was being discarded.

'We were,' Martina said.

'I wish I knew more about astronomy,' I said, trying to put an edge of menace in my voice. 'I have so many questions. Bruno lives across the courtyard, yes?'

'Yes,' Arnau said, walking to the windows and looking out. It was a warm morning, but Martina had not opened the doors, and I had not asked her.

'So you *are* in a little club,' I said.

'And now, so are you,' Arnau said. 'Don't worry, the club is quite harmless. A handful of enthusiasts. Passens built a marvel here, and we honour that achievement, and we keep it to ourselves. Will you join us in that trust?'

I had my thoughts on this, and might have shared them, but Martina replied at once. 'Yes. Of course. *Desde luego.*'

'Martina . . .' I said.

'This is my home,' she said to me.

Arnau turned from the window, beaming. 'I am so pleased. I thought you would fit in. It is always difficult to judge when to . . . help newcomers understand. Young people tend not to stay in one place for long, you know? Always rushing, rushing. And you would be amazed how few think to stop and look at the stars!'

'And what,' I said, 'are we looking at?'

'Coma Berenices, naturally,' Arnau said. 'Although, let us say, from a different perspective. And you have chosen a fortuitous moment to begin your observations. We have been watching for a . . . particular wonder.'

He would not elaborate further and made his excuses. After his departure, I confronted Martina about her readiness to agree to secrecy.

'Like I said, this is my home,' she said. 'I like it here. The sky is different, sure. But so what? It's the sky, it's far away – a lot further away than it should be, it seems. It can't harm me. This is central Barcelona. I don't have to look.'

'You don't . . . ?' I began. 'Your plan is to *not look*?'

'I wasn't interested in the stars before,' Martina said, 'and I don't need to be interested now. Stars are stars. The flat is great. When people find a place they like, it's easy to overlook flaws.'

'Flaws!' I exclaimed. 'This isn't . . . black mould in the bathroom, or dodgy wiring!'

'That's right,' Martina said. 'Those are dangerous. And people still ignore them.'

'And what about the secret society? Will you ignore them as well?'

'Secret society?' Martina said, raising an eyebrow. 'Again with this?'

'It's a society, it's secret, it's dedicated to keeping a secret . . .'

'Harmless, Arnau said.'

'What do you expect him to say? 'We are going to *Rosemary's Baby* you'?'

She scowled at me. 'You are being silly. And you are the cause of this, by the way! Perhaps your concern is the product of a guilty conscience.'

I was about to tersely deny this when I hit the possibility that she might have a point. 'I suppose that's true. Sorry.'

'Don't be sorry,' she said, kindly. 'I appreciate the concern. And look, you were right to be intrigued. It is intriguing, more so than I imagined.'

She had stood and wandered to the window, taking Arnau's place. 'See – it's all normal now. I know that's the Barcelona sky up there. The stars only come out at night. It's fine.'

Disquiet lingered, but it was impossible to express its source or nature, so I kept it to myself.

'It doesn't seem to have done Arnau any harm,' I said. I was rationalising, I knew, but mostly for the benefit of my conscience. 'He didn't warn you off or threaten you.'

'And he's up at the top,' Martina said. 'Much more exposed, if there was anything . . . What could be more harmless than stargazing? Everything you're looking at is millions of miles away.'

'True,' I said. The only hazard I associated with amateur astronomy was getting cold.

'You're only here one more night,' she said. 'Let's watch together. A private sky, just for us – don't you think that's remarkable? And Arnau said there would be something special to see. 'A particular wonder."

This was also true. I didn't even think the vow of secrecy amounted to much – as if half a dozen elderly cranks in a Barcelona apartment building knew what I talked about in London.

◊

Arnau had no cause to worry about that. I will never breathe a word about it, not to anyone. And who would believe me if I did? No one.

I left the apartment at once. It was past one in the morning, but I did not care. I didn't even know what direction I was going, at first, I was just trying to get *away*, away from Casa Berenice, away from the courtyard, away. I wanted to be under any other sky – I wanted to be under our sky. But even then, on the night bus to the airport, I could not dare look out of the window. During my nine hours at the airport, I stayed away from even a chance glimpse upwards, and for once I was glad of my aisle seat on the plane.

Never again will I regret London's overcast and light-stained skies. Never again will I regret my ignorance of the constellations. I do not want to know where to find Coma

Berenices and its distant, dim collection of galaxies and superclusters. I have seen more of that region than most – I have seen and *been seen*.

Martina did not flee. We communicated little afterwards, but I know that she decided to stay at Casa Berenice. Arnau had been right about her.

We went out onto the balcony at about eleven, when it was properly dark, and we saw Bruno was out. He greeted us with a smile and a wave, no longer suspicious. He said nothing. I knew that Arnau was out on his balcony as well, and the others. The atmosphere was expectant, and reverent. The exotic stars were as they had been before, at a slightly different phase. The green ringed planet was rising, and again across our view was the bloody strait of a galaxy whose light would not reach the Earth until I have been dead for millions of years. For that mercy, I am grateful. It was enchanting, and we sat together and watched, sharing the binoculars, talking little.

At half past midnight, it rose. Only a sliver could be seen at first. One oddity of this alien sky, or at least a difference from our own, was the absence of a moon. That night we learned there was a moon, of sorts, much closer than our own, so at its peak it was wider than the courtyard. But I never saw it at its peak. We saw that first paring, pale like our own moon, but polished, reflecting the ruddy shine of those infernal heavens. It was uniform too, with no craters, but as more waxed across the night it revealed red striations like the canals of Mars. And then that awful centre, not a crater, not the eclipse-shadow of another object. The true horror of the object could not be grasped at first. We were slow to accept what we saw, as more and more came into

view and the reality became impossible to reject. It was an
eye, a hideous bloodshot eye, and as I know for certain I
saw it, I know for certain that it saw me.

Notes on London's Housing Crisis

DAY TO DAY, it's easy to forget that London is in the grip of a profound housing crisis. This extraordinary city remains one of the best places in the world to live, work and have fun. On the surface, the capital is prosperous, busy and happy. But gather Londoners around a dinner table and the talk will often turn to house prices. Many people have friends and family members in grim conditions that at times seem inescapable. For some of us, paying for the roof over our heads has become a treadmill. Our ability to choose where we live is retreating. Many people feel that they have been short-changed by the city.

These problems can at times appear insurmountable and inevitable: just part of the condition of London in 2016, a condition that arose in the natural course of the city's development and that we all have to accept. But the failures of London's housing supply were not inevitable. The city could have turned out very differently. It's sometimes hard to remember that; a city is an aggregation of human intentions and decisions, all of which could have gone another way.

London is always changing, but also remains very much the same place. At present I live in Camden, and from the 30th level I'm able to look out over a city that would be recognisable to a Victorian: the green expanse of Regent's Park, the silver band of the Thames, that grey-brown-yellow patchwork of brick and stucco. Even the contributions of the last century have mellowed into timeless familiarity: the Post Office tower, the cathedrals of culture on the South Bank, the great metalled hulk of Midlands East Coast Station down at King's Cross, Cedric Price's space frame over the Great Court of the British Museum, the tree strucs of Soho, Fitzrovia and Finsbury, and the far gleam of the CLR James Linear struc, winding its way through Brixton and Peckham. In the east, the sun rises behind the towers of the electronics giants – Pye, EKCO, Marconi Systems, Beer Cybnernetics – at Wapping, and glances off the wings of a wide-bodied BOAC Comet 20 as it begins its final descent into Stafford Cripps International at Cliffe.

I'm presently plugged in the Walter Sickert Housing Structure, a tree overlooking Dickens Linear. As I write, seated at the dining table in my kitchen pod, I can see some of my neighbours in Dickens are upgrading what looks like a living room. A service crane has attached itself to the old pod and, with an eruption of escaping pigeons, out it comes. Everything is automated, pushbutton; right now in the struc's control centre, or at County Hall, an operator from the GLC's housing authority might be watching blocks moving on a screen, but they don't need to do or approve anything. The crane extends, removing the pod from the ziggurat side of the struc, dangling it over the canal; then it turns sharply, transferring the pod to an access rail. The replacement pod is waiting there, clean and shiny, yet to be baptised by the London rain and pollution. Through the binoculars I can make out the brand: Conran, very chic and minimal, but a triple-width pod that has a lot of room for minimalism. It's exactly the kind of conspicuous, expensive good taste I've come to expect from Dickens Linear. Already the crane has it clamped, and repeats its just-completed actions in reverse, swinging out over Camden, then retracting to move the pod into its dock.

In a few short years we'll be celebrating the 50th anniversary of the first strucs – half a century in which we have been able to take this kind of endless flexibility for granted. Or rather, half a century of being promised total flexibility and finding that the reality doesn't quite live up to the pledge. Still, it's a system with remarkable strengths. Plug and live is only a couple of grand for a starter set, easy terms, manageable even if you're on nothing more than the UBI. Upgrade your rooms as you please, as plainly or as expensively as you please. Nothing to pay but the rent on your docks. And, if you tire of your neighbourhood, move house. Every pod you own can be moved to any SLOC in Greater London within 12 hours. Push-button arrangements. Wake up in Camden, get on the Bennet, book your new docks, go to the pub, and go to bed in Blackheath. Think! Don't drink and reSLOC. Remember where you docked your home.

But those neighbours of mine, down there in Dickens Linear – when did they last reSLOC? That living room of theirs is triple-width – their whole SLOC must be ten docks, double-width kitchen, double-width bedrooms, who knows what other extra bolt-ons. A top-level view out over the city, but it's a linear, so they can be on the train, Tube or Ringway in no time. If I had a SLOC like that I might never move. But I probably won't get one – because people like them will never move. And it's nice to be able to afford a Conran living-room set every three years. On the UBI plus a writer's pay I'm stuck with a basic Ikea 'Konstant' living-room pod I bought in 2010. Its growing shabbiness would be bad enough, but I'm way behind on the operating software upgrades. It's prone to glitching in the lights and hifi, and more embarrassing afflictions. Imagine having girlfriends over to 'Ceefax & chill', only for their new Pyephone to pick up something nasty from the defective Bennet firewall. Meanwhile, dock rents continue to rise – some people have to pay more than £200 a month just for a three-bed home in central London. This is the present reality. For a few, housing costs are nudging towards an intolerable 20% of their household budget. It's worth taking a step back and understanding how we ended up in this state.

After the Second World War, housing was in huge demand across the developed world, and was accordingly built in vast quantities. To begin with, this new housing was designed exclusively along pre-War lines, as individual surface houses and apartment blocks. Some of these were constructed using novel techniques, and along modernist aesthetic lines, but typologically there was not a great deal of advance. But come the late 1950s and early 1960s, architects and designers were thinking more radically, and proposing continuous serviced frames into which mass produced home units could be plugged and unplugged.

The home could thus be liberated from the vagaries of the building site – it would no longer have to be 'built' at all, but instead could be mass-produced in factories, completely standardised. Cars and consumer goods were being made that way, said the pioneers, why not homes? The giant structures into which these consumer-friendly homes could be inserted would be very expensive to build, at first, but this was balanced out by the tumbling cost of the residential pods.

'Struc' housing of this kind was proposed by myriad architects including Archigram in the UK, Paul Rudolph in the USA and the Metabolists in Japan, and many others in Europe and the Communist bloc. On four continents, famous designers were clamouring for the same (or at least highly similar) technology. In retrospect, that gives the struc an air of inevitability. If it hadn't been tried in New York, surely it would have been tried in Tokyo; if not in Tokyo, then in London, surely.

No, not surely. Very little is truly inevitable – least of all an extraordinary breakthrough like the struc. The first experiments in the form were vastly expensive and desperately open to failure. Success had numerous preconditions: manufacturers taking up the idea, consumers adapting to a new way of thinking about their home, the law accommodating new forms of tenancy. My parents were surprisingly reluctant to part with their two-bedroom, trad house in Ladbroke Grove, even against the option of living twenty levels above the same neighbourhood in Alan Turing Linear.

It's also arguable that strucs – at least in the linear form – would not have been possible without the grandiose road building schemes that New York and London undertook in the 1970s. Today, it's as difficult to imagine London without its Ringways as it is to strip Paris of its Boulevards or Moscow of its Garden Ring. But the Ringways, and the Lower Manhattan expressways, caused widespread dismay and protest when they were announced. A twist or two of local politics, and the whole network might never have appeared – and neither would the sites of the strucs.

Nothing about the strucs was inevitable. They were the product of determination and design. To accept any situation as inevitable or natural is to ignore the decisions and the ideologies that produced it.

Nevertheless, the next stages in the story of London's housing unfold with what sounds like the click of dominos. Housing costs tumbled in the 1970s and continued to decline in the 1980s. A couple of starter pods could be had for less than £200 in the first struc sections, a cost deliberately kept low to encourage uptake – and it worked. By the time the subsidies were withdrawn, production of pods had scaled up, and the entry prices stayed low. Even without starter deal, there was by then a lively market in second-hand pods. It is, just as the early prophets said, very much like buying a car: your first one is unlikely to be brand new. But unlike buying a car, a pod doesn't need an engine to provide shelter. What no one expected was the junked pods, stripped of struc certification, would still accommodate a few free spirits off-struc. Pop it on the back of a lorry, take it out to the plotlands of Essex or Kent, and live for free.

The growing availability of the new struc option drove down the price of other housing. In the first part of the century, 'home ownership' had been a considerable marker of status. More than that, for people like my parents, having a house rooted in place in the dirt, unchanging apart from in the unappealing way they decay, symbolised a kind of security and solidity that it's now hard to understand. In retrospect, it's obvious that housing should be as flexible as your living circumstances, and should easily grow or adapt to your changing family. The trad house is as ill-fitting and out-of-date as the Victorian frock coat. Imagine having to 'move house' in the old-fashioned sense: disposing of all your rooms at the same time for an entirely new set, and having to move all your possessions at once.

But of course, it was unlikely to be a move to a 'new' house – just another old one. And that's what really worked against the trad house: its expense. In earlier times, the cost of running a traditionally built home – maintaining all that dead plaster and inadequate wiring and hopeless plumbing – was offset by the accumulation of capital in the form of mortgage equity. With the strucs holding down house prices, and the banks chasing more lucrative short-term pod credit and losing interest in long-term mortgage credit on crumbling, depreciating assets, surface housing began to be a burden. The dilapidated, half-empty terraces of London we know today are the result.

If you're a middle-class bohemian or an architect, and you don't mind rotting floorboards or the smell of damp (and the associated bills), then there's rich pickings to be had from London's traditional housing stock. Hackney or Hammersmith council will give you a two-bed house in a terrace for five hundred quid, and be grateful to you. Ironically, this gives some Londoners the kind of flexibility that was once the preserve of struc-dwellers. Mobility within the strucs is dropping. During the 1980s, Londoners reSLOCed on average every four months, fully enjoying the freedom that the struc's designers imagined. That was certainly the way it was when I had my first couple of units, straight out of university. You'd reSLOC for a week, just to be near a friend's place for their birthday party, so you didn't have far to go home. You might reSLOC to be nearer a girlfriend on a third or fourth date. Today, Londoners reSLOC on average once every fourteen months. Desirable docks, such as the top level of Dickens Linear, overlooking Regent's Park, are increasingly subject to 'camping', in which owners simply refuse to relocate. While perfectly legal, this is seen as being at odds with the spirit of the housing structures, and a reduction of their overall value. For sure, I keep a close eye on the top decks of Dickens, biding my time, hoping to be away from the Sickert's rather eccentric lifts – but if slots ever open up, I never see them. I'm not organised enough. Sometimes it's tempting to look into that 'sniping' software you can get, which will jump in and reSLOC to a location of your choice as soon as it becomes available. In popular linear stretches, vacancy times are down to seconds. We know it happens, and it's technically legal, but most people consider it cheating.

Even less acceptable is 'multi-SLOCing', as increasingly practised by the wealthier and slyer struc residents: keeping multiple pod-clusters occupying docks in different locations. It used to be that even the most dedicated 'campers' would want to reSLOC eventually – for instance to enjoy a couple of weeks living in Brighton in the summer. But now they might keep a cluster year-round in a desirable

SLOC by the seaside and simply travel there. Last year, County Hall announced it was looking into regulating multi-SLOCing, but it's hard to see how it can without introducing more bureaucracy and oversight into a system that is founded on simplicity and freedom. If I ever do luck into a SLOC on top of the Dickens, I'd be unlikely to want to let it go – so maybe I can't blame those neighbours of mine too much.

Meanwhile, costs are rising. Struc construction has slowed significantly since the beginning of the 21st century. In the thirty years to 2000, the number of available docks rose on average 30 percent every year. That pace of expansion could not, of course, be kept up indefinitely. The construction of the Ringway network – which cleared the ground for the Linears – was officially completed in 1991, and there are no serious plans for further expansion. The only Linear built since then followed the route of the high-speed rail link from the Channel Tunnel into Concorde Station, and after the delays and disputes that accompanied that project, there's little appetite for a reprise. Meanwhile, we are running out of appropriate sites for tree strucs. The central canopy is completed, and there are few opportunities for infill additions. Outside Ringway 1, there are thousands of hectares of under-populated, dilapidated surface housing that can yield sites, but not at a pace that can meet demand. Meanwhile an increasing proportion of the GLC Housing Authority's budget is taken up with maintenance and emergency repairs. With both cost areas expected only to rise, finance for new strucs is tightening.

As dock supply fails to keep pace with rising demand, Londoners are also having to upgrade their rooms more often to keep pace with improvements in information technology. The average family used to upgrade its living room once every five years. That has now dropped to once every three years. My new Pyephone 12 simply refuses to connect with the command software in my Ikea living room and Hotpoint kitchen – and good luck trying to get a ten-year-old pod to connect to the Bennet at all.

What can be done? More strucs are plainly needed, particularly near the Docklands, Park Royal and Stratford thinkbelts, where most of London's new jobs are created. At the same time, the bright young things in those thinkbelts need to work less on the latest apps and gadgets, and more on making durable open-source strucware that won't simply glitch up within four years. In the meantime, perhaps pressure on the system can be eased by encouraging more people to live in traditional housing.

This might take effort. Trad housing is rightly seen as shabby, inconvenient and a bottomless money pit. However, if demand for surface housing can be increased just a little, a virtuous circle might result. The value of the old-fashioned houses and flats might begin to rise a little. This would be a welcome windfall for the owners, and in the long term might even amount to something like an investment. This rising value would give the owners an incentive to repair and improve their properties to further boost their value. If a trad house stopped being a miserable drain on resources, it might become more desirable, attracting more house-buyers and further raising prices. For a time, in the late 1950s and early 1960s, rising house prices were seen as a normal feature of what was then called a 'housing market'. It will be strange to see the provision of a basic need – shelter – as a 'market' with 'investments' and 'appreciation', rather than purely a technological, industrial matter of consistently exceeding demand. Utopian, even. But there was a time when mass produced housing and residential megastructures were also seen as utopian and impractical, rather than the stuff of everyday life.

I'm prepared to do my part. Right now, I'm looking at a three-bedroom terraced house in Notting Hill – not the best neighbourhood, but Kensington & Chelsea only wants £675 to be rid of it. It'll cost maybe five times that to fix everything that's wrong with it, but I'm treating that as a new hobby. Next week I'll trade in my Sickert SLOC and binoculars for a toolbox and some plaster. It doesn't even have a Bennet connection – I expect to spend the next six months on the phone to the Post Office sorting that out. Back to the ground level. I don't know if my parents would be proud, or appalled.

Moths

M Y BROTHER, AS the eldest, took on the really big jobs: arranging my father's funeral and executing the will. My sister, the middle child, was responsible for clearing out Dad's house.

I thought I got off lightly. Then I realised I had been stitched up – a classic conspiracy against the guileless youngest child. To me fell the task of sorting the photographs. Sure, I said. No problem. Are you sure that's all you want me to do?

There would be a lot of photos, I was never in any doubt about that. Dad was an enthusiastic photographer. At every family event, on every outing, he had his camera in his hand. A succession of cameras, in fact. For most of our childhood he wielded an Olympus Trip 35, but in the 21st century he became an early adopter and worked through a variety of improving models of digital camera. Despite early and eager conversion to digital technology, he remained loyal to making prints. During the Olympus era, he had briefly tried setting up a dark room in the attic, but he found it too much hassle. And I think he liked the ritual of taking the little rolls of used film to Snappy Snaps, waiting three days, and then picking up the envelopes of photos. In later years, when the local Snappy Snaps became a nail bar, and then a Foxtons, he invested in a home photo printer, which achieved pretty good results. But I don't think it was quite the same for him as the to-and-fro of depositing and collecting; even the wait time was important. The delayed gratification made everything more satisfying.

Photography was, for Dad, a documentary pursuit. He wasn't interested in art. The aim was to make an accurate record of an event. When something came out wrong – wonky, or saturated with pink alien light, or double-exposed – he would say, 'Oh, very arty.' He didn't mean it as praise. He liked everything squarely in frame, everyone smiling, everyone's eyes open, everything in focus. But only the worst duds, the total failures, the unbroken fields of black or white or velvety grey, would be thrown away. He also would throw away anything that attracted one of those oval advice stickers from the lab, which he regarded as patronising in the extreme. I think that was the basis of his feud with the photo studio at Boots the chemist – the staff at Snappy Snaps knew him better. But misfires, badly composed or blurry shots, fatally 'arty' efforts, would still be kept. It pained him to throw away prints. They cost money, after all. In every envelope from the lab, you would get an index print showing thumbnails of all the photos in the batch, and I think he regarded that like a Panini sticker album: it was important to have a full set.

Christmas and Easter. Summer holidays. Five birthdays a year, not counting my grandparents when they were still with us, and occasional round numbers with uncles, aunts and cousins. Three school plays a year. Some significant wedding anniversaries. Outings, so many outings. You see how it adds up.

After Mum died four years ago, the photography tailed off. Everything tailed off. Had it been about her, all the time? He kept a photograph Blu-Tac'd inside the little bureau he used as a desk at home: Mum, in the mid 1970s, before any of us were born, sitting on a grassy slope with her knees up, a wide unguarded smile on her face, and a strand of brown hair blowing across her eyes, which are closed. Quite an 'arty' shot, now I think about it, but it was without a doubt Dad's favourite. By the mid 1990s, this exposure had faded quite badly, and Dad was able to find the correct negative and make a new print. That was an unanswerable vindication of his photo-hoarding, and afterwards there was no question of him throwing anything away.

So, I knew there would be a lot of photographs, but how bad could it be?

'You've got your work cut out for you,' my sister said with a slight smirk when I met her at the house a few days after the funeral.

'There are the boxes in the guest room,' I said. The smallest bedroom had been used as a dumping ground for a while, and I knew that the four or five boxes in the corner behind my brother's keyboard stand had photos in them.

'Yup, there are those boxes. And some more in Dad's bedroom. A couple by the bureau. There were some in the attic as well.'

'Oh, right,' I said.

'I've found fourteen boxes in total,' she said, again with that little sly smile. 'How long are you staying?'

'I thought I might spend an afternoon on it,' I said.

'An *afternoon*?' she said. Her amusement was gone.

Efficient to a fault, my sister had already cleared most of the house. The boxes of photos were stacked together in the living room, along with a few pieces of furniture I was taking, and a couple of boxes that I had already filled with keepsakes and childhood things.

'It's a big job,' she said.

'Yeah,' I said. I swallowed. 'You know . . . I wonder if we might be able to dump a couple of these boxes, sight unseen. I mean . . . We're not planning to keep every photo, are we? Lots are going to end up getting chucked. So we could just . . . lighten the load . . .'

'*Lighten the load*?' my sister said acidly. '*Lighten the load*?'

'You've thrown away loads of stuff,' I said. 'And I saw the boxes that went to charity – twenty, thirty boxes?'

'I went through everything first!' she said, crossing her arms angrily. 'I wasn't disposing of anything 'sight unseen'! I was here every day for a week! I took time off work! And the stuff that went to charity – who wants a load of old *National Geographic*s and Giles albums? A broken microwave? These are family photographs we're talking about.'

'OK, OK,' I said. 'Sorry. You've worked really hard.'

'Look, I know you're probably going to end up with . . . like . . . forty or fifty murky pictures of the *Mary Rose*,' she said. 'God, how many times did we go to see that bloody boat? Three?'

'Twice, for me,' I said.

'And there was a time before you were born. Anyway. I know that's all going in the bin. But those photos meant something to Dad. We should respect that, and give them a bit of time.'

'Yeah. Sure.'

Efficient, fair-minded and generally in the right – just a few of my sister's numerous personality flaws.

'And, who knows what you'll find in there,' she said. 'Maybe some real treasure.'

◊

An afternoon certainly wasn't enough time. And my sister wanted to finish the clear-out so the house could go on the market. She was already planning to courier the bits of furniture I wanted, so she booked a slightly bigger van and the fourteen boxes arrived at my flat the following week.

'How long are they going to be there?' my partner asked once the boxes were piled in the corner of our living room.

'They're not staying,' I said. 'There probably won't be enough to fill a box when I'm done. I've just got to crack on with it.'

'Hmm, well,' my partner said. 'Better get cracking.'

Dad had made one effort to sort out the photographs, last year. 'I'm going to sort out the boxes,' he said, more than once, in the months prior. They were weighing on his conscience as his health faltered. When I visited, I saw he had stripped the bed in the little guest room and had started to empty one of the boxes onto the bare mattress.

The next time I visited, three or four weeks later, the scene was exactly the same. How's it going, I asked. His face clouded. 'It's a big job,' he said, and there was an evasive quality in this reply that meant I didn't pursue it.

I thought I understood: too much Mum. Fair enough. On the next visit, the guest room bed had been made up again, and the boxes were back as they had been.

The weekend after the boxes arrived, I got cracking. I thought – hoped – that Dad's foray into the boxes had imposed some kind of organisational spine. Alas, no. One box had '1988-89' written on it in confident marker pen, but contained packets of photos spanning at least two decades. Another was inscribed 'Family Hols', and the first packet I withdrew had pictures from Mum's retirement party. Unsure where or how to begin, it occurred to me that the box Dad had tried to sort out himself might contain clues – I was hoping for some kind of index or detailed instructions, though I knew it was unlikely, but any guidance at all would be welcome.

I found the wine box that Dad had emptied onto the bed – one of those boxes that fit six bottles, and which are such a convenient size for storing books and photographs. And the contents did show some promising signs of organisation. Many of the photographs had been taken out of their Snappy Snaps wallets and were in undifferentiated bundles at the bottom of the box. I picked out one of these bundles, which was wrapped with an A4 sheet of paper and cinched by a rubber band. On the paper, my father had written DISCARD.

That was clear enough. I put the bundle to one side, and did the same with the others. They amounted to about two-thirds of the weight of the box. Good job, Dad.

What remained in the Snappy Snaps wallets was well chosen. A Christmas in the early 1990s, judging from the *Dances With Wolves* VHS Mum was holding up. Me and

my sister visiting a steam fair, my brother old enough to
opt out. Mum and Dad in Barcelona at the end of the
Millennium.

I assume it was Mum *and* Dad, anyway. Mum was
certainly there, and someone was behind the camera. One
persistent feature of these photographs was the absence of
Dad. Mum, of course, was inescapable. In fact, I could hear
Dad's voice, urging her to be in the shot, and I could hear
her modest demurrals and equally modest acquiescence.
Funny how, if a scene is repeated often enough, the dead
can recreate it in your mind's eye – not memory, exactly,
but a faithful simulation. We children were slightly less
essential – my sister and I were outnumbered by steam
engines in the saved photos. But Dad, of course, was out
of shot, wielding the apparatus. When he relinquished the
camera, the results were not ideal. A picture from Spain
showed the problem. Mum and Dad seated on the terrace
of a restaurant, white plastic table covered in a red cloth,
the ruins of a good meal, a pergola covered in vines. The
camera has evidently been given to a waiter or another
patron. Mum is laid-back and convivial, with an easy smile,
raising her glass. Dad is leaning forward, tense, mouth a
little open, his left hand slightly blurred by movement, his
eyes fixed on a point just above the lens. I was not present,
but I know what he is doing: he is delivering a stream of
instructions to the person taking the photo, and he will not
relax until the camera is back in his hands.

This was not how he looked in life, but it was how
he generally looked in photos. He did not trust camera
timers, fellow tourists, helpful passers-by and hotel staff.
Not with this sacred duty, in any case. He liked the rise of

phone cameras – the mass compulsion to document was a phenomenon he recognised – but he did not understand 'selfies'. It wasn't that he thought them vain – they just seemed pointless. To Dad, the camera was a device that pointed outward.

As such, I found very few pictures of Dad – only two, in fact in that whole box. My rough plan had been to divide the photos into four piles: one pile for each sibling, and one for the bin. Sorry Dad, but we did not need quite so many pictures from an unremembered steam fair – not the ones that didn't contain any family members. And it was now clear to be that it was the presence of family members – or the scenery of home – that made a photo worth keeping, not interesting examples of obsolete agricultural machinery.

So, here's a photo of uncle Glenn, visiting us at Christmas in 1991, or 1992, sitting on the sofa, cup of tea. It's a nice photo of him, his mouth half-open and asymmetric with amusement, clearly in the middle of a conversation with Dad while Dad takes the picture. Glenn died in 2011. But the domestic details are just as precious: the hideous rumpled William Morris covers Mum made for the sofa and armchairs so they'd match (they didn't match); the British Telecom mug that Glenn is holding, from Dad's work; the Nintendo Entertainment System cartridges just visible on the hearth rug in the corner of the frame. These details made the photo well worth keeping.

But it was just that one photo, and the two of Dad. And, in the batch of photos from that Christmas, the same was true of other relatives. Only one photo of Grandpa Mike, with his back mostly to the camera, laying cutlery on the dining table. Only two photos of my other grandparents,

on Mum's side, taken on a walk near their house during a
visit in the days after Christmas.

Why so few? Dad never just took one photo. They
were fired off in threes and fours, 'for safety'. I went from
applauding my father's stack of discards to wondering if
maybe he had gone too far. It was possible he reasonably
thought one photo of uncle Glenn was enough, but ideally
I wanted three, one for each of his children. My brother
and sister could discard them if they wanted, but I wasn't
going to be faulted on fairness. I was the youngest child.
Everything had to be fair.

With a sinking heart, feeling that I was taking a step
backwards, I unwrapped one of the discard bundles Dad
had made, and began flipping through to find duplicates of
uncle Glenn and my grandparents. Dad's work had been
pretty thorough, and his instincts had been pretty good.
I found twenty of more photos of engines at the steam
fair, many of them indistinguishable from the dozen or
so he had kept, some crooked or blurry or obscured by
smudges. Almost at once I found more pictures of uncle
Glenn, taken in the same moment as the retained one.
Sofa, British Telecom mug, hearth rug; Glenn with his
head slightly raised and his eyes half-closed; Glenn with
his head lowered, mouth wider, and eyes mostly closed;
Glenn with head slightly turned and elbow lifting off the
arm of the sofa. Put these together in the right order and
you could make a little flip-book animation of my late
uncle mid-sentence. You could practically lip-read him.
And Dad had picked the best one. A faint, ragged daub
covered quite a lot of the exposure in one shot, leaching the
colour and detail from the ugly William Morris sofa cover,

a chemical fault in the developing process. But in one of the other discards there was an extra feature. Over Glenn's shoulder, you could see the doorway into the kitchen, and there was an extra figure, a hunched back, in silhouette – Mike, most likely, passing through.

A spasm of pain interrupted me. I was sitting cross-legged on the living room floor, and my leg had cramped. Gasping and swearing, I clambered onto my feet and hopped about, trying to get the pain to go and normal feeling to come back, cursing the advance of middle age.

On my feet, and not wanting to sit down again, I limped through to the kitchen.

'You OK?' my partner said.

'Cramp,' I said.

'How's it going?' she asked.

Well, so far I'm un-discarding photos from the discard pile, I did not say.

'Fine,' I said. 'Cracking on.'

Wanting to give my trip to the kitchen a constructive appearance, I opened the bottom drawer used for miscellaneous items and started to rummage. Garden twine (we have no garden), light bulbs that may or may not work, mystery keys, egg cups for the boiled eggs we never eat.

'What are you looking for?' my partner asked.

'Magnifying glass,' I said. 'I want to identify who's in that photo. That's my uncle Glenn holding the mug, but I don't know who the other person is.'

I had left the Glenn photos on the kitchen table. She picked one up.

'Huh,' she said. 'What a weird effect. Double exposure?'

Magnifying glass in hand, I turned to the table. 'Double exposure? What? The person in the kitchen.'

'I don't see anyone in the kitchen. I see a man sitting next to your uncle.'

I frowned. The photo with the silhouette in the kitchen was on the table. She was looking at the photo with the strange, desaturated smear across it.

'That's not a person,' I said. 'It's a . . . chemical screw-up of some kind during developing.'

'No, look, it's a person,' she said. 'Head. Legs, there. And the arm of the sofa cuts in front of it.'

Taking the photo from her, I squinted at the smear, and looked at it through the lens.

'It can't be a person,' I said. 'You can see the pattern on the fabric through it.'

'Double exposure, like I said. Someone was sitting there in one photo, and got up and left, but the same section of film was exposed . . .'

'If that was the case the whole image would be oversaturated,' I said. 'And these photos are in a series, not even seconds apart, there's no time for someone to get up and leave. It doesn't make sense.'

But she was right: the discoloured marking had the distinct outline of a person sitting on the sofa next to Glenn, closer to the camera.

'Maybe it's a ghost,' she said, deadpan. 'That's how they faked a lot of those ghost photos: double exposure.'

'It's not a ghost,' I snapped.

'All right, all right,' my partner said, backing off with her hands raised. 'Only kidding.'

I was being tetchy to cover my disquiet, but I meant

what I said. Of course it wasn't a ghost. The bleached look of the smear, the nimbus of grapefruit pink at the edges — it was a mishap in the developing process, it all had that synthetic sheen.

'Sorry,' I said. 'I've been spending too much time with the dead.'

◊

Cramp gone, I returned to the photos. The smudge in the Glenn photo was not a one-off, I knew — I had noticed, but passed over, a similar flaw in other prints. Flipping back through the discards, I came across another almost immediately: me, sitting in the driver's seat of a team tractor; my sister standing on the ground facing the camera, a serious expression on her face. And beside her a long strip of discolouration, again with that coral aura. A mark left by a roller in a processing machine, I thought at first glance. But looking at it again, I saw the proportions of a person, an arm stretched out across my sister's shoulders.

A fifth pile was formed, containing instances of this anomaly, which Dad had discarded. There were more than forty in all, spread across every role of film, covering every decade and location. A few were no more than a shapeless blob, or just a blush of salmon-tinted over-saturation. But in most, the rough outline of a person could be inferred.

It was not a ghost, that was for sure. No ghost would follow my father wherever he went, posing for pictures. It was a recurring lapse in the taking or developing of the photographs — nothing else could explain such a consistent effect. But it troubled me.

Most disquieting was a second photo from the
Barcelona holiday, a twin of the snap of Mum and Dad
in the restaurant – the helpful waiter, or fellow diner, had
fired off a couple. Here was a much better photo of Dad,
more at ease, smiling, not trying to correct something in
the photographer's technique. And behind him – where
the other photo had contained only the blackness of night
with a few scattered points of light – there was the patch
of distortion. It ended neatly at the edge of the table, as if
standing behind it, and again one of its 'arms' was curled
out around my father's shoulders, disappearing behind his
neck and then reappearing on his polo shirt. This was very
precise for a random chemical flub.

Dad had seen this photo. He had seen it when trying
to sort out the boxes, and he had discarded it in favour
of the worse picture of himself – presumably because of
this glitch. He didn't like the glitch. I sympathised, and I
suspected I knew why he had abandoned his own effort
to sort out the boxes.

Still, I persevered, filial duty and whatnot. I cracked
into a second box, and a third, and carved the contents into
piles: for me, for my brother, for my sister, discard, and . . .
defective. The discard pile should have been the biggest –
but it was rivalled by the defective photos, containing the
development anomaly.

I wished I could ask my father what it was. Perhaps he
knew and could explain it, and I would be embarrassed at
this crawling unease. Or perhaps he did not know; perhaps
he had faced, in his last years, this same unnamed fear that
I now felt. Grief is like water – we only really feel it when
it's in motion, moving across our surfaces. When we want

to ask a question, and remember we can't. When we wish we had known something, or said something, and cannot.

◊

Dad wasn't around to ask, but there were others who might know. Near my flat in east London was a photo studio, clinging on to business through the 21st century by making prints of digital pictures, taking family portraits, and meeting the very precise requirements for passports and visas. I had been in before, to get physical duplicates of phone pictures of my niece when she was a newborn. It was a cluttered place filled with frame samples, SD cards for sale, faded personalised mugs, and weird promotional objects that could be made in cubes of lucite or glass. But the grey in the moustache of the Bengali proprietor, and the laboratory tang in the air, had the promise of expertise. On Monday I went there with an envelope of defective photos. I also took some of the nicer family snaps I had found, intending to order duplicates and blow-ups, not wanting to avail myself of the proprietor's expertise without paying for something.

To his credit, Murad treated my errand with full seriousness. He studied the smeared prints under strong light, and he looked at them through a loupe.

'Do you have the negatives?' he asked.

Embarrassingly, I hadn't considered bringing the negatives for the defective prints. But fortunately the envelope I used to carry them had a few in an inside pocket. My Mum's parents' ruby wedding, the mid 1980s; aunt Hannah, in a long floral dress, carrying a glass of white wine. Beside her, partly obscuring a wisteria-covered wall, the . . . defect.

Murad examined this print and compared it to the corre-
sponding negative, which he placed on a lightbox.

'Yes,' he said, as if confirming a hypothesis. He gestured
me to look through the loupe. 'See. It's not on the negative.'

'Oh,' I said. 'What does that mean? An error in
processing?'

'Hmm,' Murad said. He was studying the exposure
again. 'Not really. These are all from different times, yes?
They were stored together?'

'Yes,' I said. 'It's a storage problem? They've been
damaged somehow? They were in boxes, away from light,
all dry . . .'

'In boxes, yes, packed away, forgotten, no one looking
at them?'

'Not *forgotten*, exactly,' I said, feeling a little defensive,
although I could not tell exactly why.

'Vermin.'

'Excuse me?'

'It is a kind of vermin,' Murad said. 'Not common, but
not rare. In the trade we call them moths – Muybridge
moths, after Eadweard Muybridge, an early photographer.
I don't know why him. Maybe he saw them first.'

'Moths?' I said. 'But . . . it's obviously a problem with
the photograph. It's not some insect.'

'Not an insect, no,' Murad said. In a quite sudden movement, he gathered up the defective prints and stuffed them
back into the envelope. 'These should be destroyed. Did
you say you had boxes of these?'

'Fourteen boxes,' I said.

He gave me a baleful look. 'Too many. Find all the
infested prints and get rid of them.'

'Infested?' I said, alarmed. 'This is . . . alive?'

'No,' Murad said. Then he shrugged. 'I don't know. I'm not an expert. I know someone who knows more than me. He has a shop in the West End. I'll send him a message. He will have more information.'

'That's great,' I said. 'Thank you.'

Murad passed the envelope back to me and rubbed sanitiser on his hands, which I thought was overkill. 'Let's have a look at these duplicates.'

I gave him the other envelope. He took the prints out and laid them in front of him.

'This is from the others, I think,' he said, holding one up. My eighth or ninth birthday – all five of us seated on or around the sofa in the living room (William Morris covers slightly less rumpled at this earlier date), me proudly holding a dinosaur Transformers toy (Grimlock). The camera must have been put on a timer on the sideboard, and Dad looks a bit tense about it.

Behind him was the pale smudge.

'That wasn't there before,' I said. 'This was one I wanted to copy.'

Murad looked at me over the top of his glasses. 'Moths,' he said.

◊

At home, the same day, I worked in a frenzy, tearing through box after box, envelope after envelope, stripping out every single 'moth-infested' print I could find. I didn't hesitate over any of them, no matter what was in the picture; and I didn't spare any borderline cases, where the

effect might be innocent lens flare or over-exposure. All
went into a black bin bag. I wanted to burn the bag, but
I had nowhere to do that safely, and I could imagine the
toxic plume they'd produce. The outside bin would have
to do. The thought of infestation – of something stealthily
eating its way through photo after photo – was disgusting
to me. And I had seen it spread. If I failed to act, I feared
the whole of Dad's archive might be lost.

At the same time, the moths, whatever they were, fasci-
nated me. I had never encountered anything like them,
and what little Murad could tell me was intriguing. They
were not noisome like the specks of black mould that attack
photos and papers that get damp; indeed, they were not
attacking the pictures from the outside at all, but somehow
from within. The glossy surface of the print was undisturbed, as was its silky back. The moth was not in the
physical material of the photograph but in its information,
in the content of the picture. They inserted themselves
into scenery, behind objects, and they sought out human
subjects. Indeed, I found very few in photos without
humans present. And why did they take humanoid form?

I found myself studying prints that contained the clear-
est 'moths' trying to make sense of them. And I could not
part with the bin bag, not before I knew more about them.
I wished I had asked Murad for the details of his expert
colleague, rather than relying on him getting in touch.

Fortunately, I did not have to wait long. Three days
after I went to the photo lab, I received a phone call from
a man introducing himself as Gareth at Fitzrovia Classic
Photographic.

'I understand you have affective artefacts,' he said.

There was a patrician, doctorly tone to his voice that I found utterly reassuring. 'A bad case.'

'Effective . . . ?' I said. 'You mean the moths? Muybridge moths?'

Was that a faint sigh at the other end of the line? 'Affective artefacts, to be precise. Muybridge called them nyxotypes. Moth is shorthand. How many?'

'I've filled a bin bag.'

The sigh was much more distinct this time. 'That is a bad case. What was the source?'

'Of the moths – the, er, artefacts?'

'Of the photos.'

I described my father's compulsive photography, and the fourteen boxes.

'Oh dear,' Gareth said. 'Really you should get rid of them all.'

'That's not possible,' I said. 'I made promises to family about them. There's an emotional dimension.'

A dry chuckle. 'Well, naturally. An emotional dimension! Nicely put. That's the trouble, you see. Photographs – photos of loved ones, anyway – carry an emotional residue. They are taken with an expectation of future feeling, like a static charge. When that is not discharged, and when those photos amass in great numbers, in darkness, the problem compounds. It becomes feedstock for this . . . phenomenon.'

'Are you saying,' I said, 'that these moths are a product of my father's *repressed emotions*?'

'I have no idea what your father did with his emotions,' Gareth said, again sounding like a GP quashing a patient's suggestion. 'I am describing what causes the affliction you reported. Muybridge thought they were caused by darkness, hence nyxotype. But that is only one component, and hardly the most important. The emotional dimension, as you put it, is the key.'

Momentarily dumbstruck, I tried to get a grip on what I had learned.

'If this . . . issue arises when photos are not looked at, will looking at the photos stop its spread?' I asked. 'That's what I'm doing now, looking at the photos, appreciating them, and I'll be sending them to my brother and sister to enjoy – won't that put a stop to it?'

A thoughtful growl. 'That's good. It'll stop fresh outbreaks. But once the infestation is established, it will continue to spread, and the affected prints can't be saved, they must be disposed of.'

'What if I don't?'

It took Gareth a couple of seconds to reply, as if he couldn't follow the question.

'Why wouldn't you?' he said. 'If you don't, they will continue to spread, and more of your photos will be ruined. You need to stop the rot.'

◊

I should have listened to him. But the moths did not seem dangerous to me. And their affective nature, their connection to unfulfilled feeling – the emotional purpose that had driven my father to take so many photographs – meant I could not simply destroy the moth-eaten prints. Surely, I reasoned, there were other ways of stopping the spread. I disposed of a great many pictures, thousands in all – but some of the better moths I retained, safely away from the unaffected prints, held in a fire-proof metal document box I bought from Rymans.

By 'better', I mean those prints where the human outline of the moth was most distinct. And those, I sometimes like to look at, marvelling at this curiosity of nature, of un-nature. I think they appreciate this attention, after all those long years incubating in the dark. Their boundaries have furred with fractal detail; the coral and grapefruit pinks of their aura have become richer. I can't see the harm in it. Although, it's true, when I picture my father now, I cannot see him without that suggestive blur at his shoulder, a little stronger every time.

Deeds

'ANYONE CAN BUILD an office block,' Napier said, 'but we want to do more than that. We want to make an authentic contribution to the fabric of the city. We want to make this a place, a real place. Not just an address.'

'Yes, I see,' Horton said. 'I mean, it's written on the wall behind you.'

Napier turned to look at the wall of the conference room, where the words 'Not just great addresses . . . Real places' had been stencilled on the exposed brick by a very exciting young street artist from Central St Martin's. 'Haha, yes,' he said. 'The writing's on the wall. But that really shows how important placemaking is to us here at Harbinger Commercial. It's at the heart of everything we do. St Synnove Gate is really the apotheosis of that. We want to make this building a new City landmark, of course, but we also want it to be a cultural event. We had such a fantastic programme of arts events at the old building, Synnove House, I don't know if you were familiar with it . . . ?'

Horton shook his head.

'NHS offices, built in the 1960s, very dark and gloomy,

but we had artists take it over and brighten it up: danc-
ers, storytelling afternoons, really made it come alive, you
know?'

'Sure.'

'And we want the arts to be an integral part of the new
building,' Napier continued. 'Not just a place to work – a
place to be inspired, a place to imagine, a place to dream.'

'Quite a lot to ask of an office building,' Horton said.

Napier laughed. He had not sat down since Horton
had arrived, as he had once heard on a podcast that sitting
down in a meeting with another man betrayed a number
of undesirable traits, and although he couldn't recall the
details, the thing about not sitting down had really stuck
with him. Horton, he noted, had sat down immediately,
but he was a writer. Restless, buoyed up by enthusiasm
for the project and eager to pass it on to his guest, Napier
turned his attention to the model of St Synnove Gate in
the middle of the conference table.

'This is just indicative, to get things moving with the
planners,' he said, giving the model a sweep of the hand
that was both dismissive and loving. 'But it gives a flavour.
On the ground floor here, next to the retail offer, we were
thinking a gallery and events space. But we want the arts
to play an even more integral part than that. I don't know,
a pattern on the facade or something like that. So it's not
just a marketing thing, it's more than that. We're hoping
that tenants see that we're really serious about culture, and
that's what makes them choose us over our competitors.'

'Yes, I see,' Horton said. 'Not marketing at all. And you
want me to write a short story about this building? This
building which hasn't even been designed?'

Napier smiled. 'Yes.'

'What for?'

'You don't want to do it?'

'For two grand? Of course I want to do it. But why do you want it?'

Feeling that it might give him an air of gravitas, Napier pulled out a chair and sat. 'It's a creative exercise for the team here. A way of getting the ideas flowing. In the past we've found it really helpful to ask novelists like yourself to write a little story, something unexpected, which can spark the imagination.'

Horton grimaced and thrust his hands into his hair, further disrupting what was already a very unruly thatch. 'Yeah, OK, but . . . you've read my novels?'

'Of course. *London Curses*. *Northern Outfall*. And *Blightchapel*. Really, uh, original and thought-provoking. We thought, you know, psychogeography – it could give the place some atmosphere.'

'But you know they're quite dark books, right? And they're not . . . They're *against* property developers, gentrification, regeneration, redevelopment, "retail offer" . . . I hate all that stuff . . . all this.'

Napier nodded. They were getting to the heart of the matter. That was why they were here in Harbinger's most creative meeting room, with the street art, and the framed black-and-white photographs of nitrous canisters in gutters by an amazing young chap at the RCA: to demonstrate that they weren't like other property developers. 'Totally. I get it. I mean, that's the point! We want to hear from outsiders, from dissidents. Something the lads – and lasses – here won't encounter as part of their day-to-day . . . Something, you know, a bit weird and dark, like your stuff . . . if you could do something along those lines, that'd be really great.'

For a long and slow moment, Horton appeared to be considering this. He was staring at the model, his brow furrowed. Napier was tempted to speak, to keep up the sales pitch, but he suspected that a creative process might be underway and he did not want to interfere.

'Place making,' Horton said at last.

Thinking that the author might be about to say more, Napier didn't respond until another silence had elapsed. 'Uh, yeah,' he said. 'Placemaking.'

'I think I get what you want,' Horton said. 'You want an added dimension. You want depth. You've got this box, this block, and it's much like any other box or block. So much floor area, climate control, branch of Leon. And you're shrewd enough to see that there's nothing very special about it. It's an empty vessel and it needs meaning.'

Napier had the feeling he was being mildly insulted, but that was to be expected from someone like Horton. And it was what they wanted. A provocateur. The grit that makes the pearl. 'Yeah, that's pretty much it. We want the added dimension that culture can bring.'

'You know what I do is fake, right?' Horton said. 'I make it up, in my head. What I do is invention, it's just affect, it's atmosphere.'

'I understand what fiction is, yes,' Napier said.

'Fiction, that's it,' Horton said, raising a finger, his eyes glittering. He had shed the jaded air he had worn through the meeting so far and become animated. 'This placemaking – it's fiction, isn't it? It's giving an invention, this new-build object, the feel of truth. Which is what I do.'

'Precisely,' Napier said, although not with total certainty. 'But . . . fiction has a truth of its own, wouldn't you say? It's not just . . . lies.'

'No, no,' Horton said gently. 'But it just feels a bit second hand. Why use my occult fabrications when you could use the real thing?'

'The real . . . ?' Napier stopped, and swallowed, fearful of appearing naive. Inviting Horton, he had expected a creative, possibly an insolent and uncooperative creative. But there was also the possibility he had brought a lunatic into Harbinger Commercial's best meeting room. 'The occult isn't real.'

Horton cracked a smile at this, and Napier was relieved to see it. 'Not real, no, but another kind of fiction, and as you say fiction has a truth to it. You want something beyond the day-to-day. Why not deal with someone who sincerely believes in the dark arts, in the psychic frame of the city, rather than an author who's just making it up?'

Napier's lips were dry and he wet them with the tip of his tongue. He could feel the disruption in the air, the sense of being unexpected, out-of-bounds. Wasn't that the purpose of this whole exercise?

'Do you know anyone like that?'

◊

Jen had written to Horton after the publication of *Blightchapel*, a letter composed in blue ballpoint on nine sheets of ruled A4 paper, with diagrams. The author emailed photos of the letter to Napier after their meeting, to give him a sense of who he was dealing with. There was no indication of a second name – Jen was the only name. She had taken issue with various aspects of Horton's novel, a time-straddling necromantic nightmare involving the tanneries that once polluted the East End.

I explained to her that it was fiction, Horton had told Napier. *And she said she knew that very well, but she wanted to give me the facts.* Afterwards, they had corresponded, and Horton had visited her. No phone, no email. Place, you see. Location. You go to her.

The address was on Whitechapel High Street, near the art gallery. Across the roaring road, one of Harbinger's competitors was building a clutch of apartment towers. But the redevelopment that had transformed Aldgate in the past decade had spared this shabby stretch of terrace, for now. At first Napier expected to end up in one of the narrow 19th-century buildings piled against each other like unread books, and he was surprised – and a little disappointed – to find it was a five-storey office from the 1950s, with a phone repair shop on the ground floor and a facade cluttered with signs for accountants and solicitors.

Her office was on the top floor. JEN, said the hand-written card by the bell and on the door, and a list of services: 'Tarot readings. Geomancy. Luck changed. Consultation on intimate matters.' Napier was aware of fringe businesses of this sort; he had evicted several from doomed industrial estates. Cards left on buses. Horton had mentioned wise women. *Maybe she's a fraud,* he had said. *Probably she is. But she's an honest fraud. She believes it.*

The office was serenaded by pneumatic drills in the street below. It smelled strongly of lemongrass incense and its ceiling tiles had been stained by a leak. One wall was devoted to a bookcase, although books were not half of what it contained: magazine racks stuffed with browning paper, antique box files with peeling labels, a Perspex box which had once adorned the shopfront of an outer London minicab office, a stuffed pigeon, aged testimonials wonky in clip frames. An IKEA sofa was covered in blankets and had been routinely slept on.

Jen sat behind a desk with her back to the window. She was not conspicuously paranormal: in later life, with cropped grey hair, wearing jeans and a black T-shirt bearing the words 'A positive attitude makes a day great'. Napier expected suspicion; the shades of all those evicted fortune-tellers on his conscience. But she did not betray any.

'St Synnove Gate,' she said, patting the brochure that Napier had sent to her ahead of the meeting. 'Farringdon. Where did you get the name?'

'There was an office block called Synnove House there,' Napier said. 'We thought St Synnove Gate had a bit of a ring to it.'

'It does,' Jen agreed, to Napier's surprise – he'd thought she would disdain that sort of branding exercise. 'Adding a saint, and a gate. Syncretic, ha. The new church adopts old prophets. Where do you think they got it from? It's Norse, or Old English – it means 'gift of the sun'. Is there any evidence of sun-worship on the site, Sunna, Mithraism . . . ?'

'Uh, not that I'm aware of. There was an archaeological survey, but it didn't turn up much, just some Roman coins, mosaic fragments, bottles, game pieces . . .'

'Remains?'

Napier raised his eyebrows. 'Human remains? Yes, but

there's nothing unusual about that. Anywhere in London, anywhere in the centre at least, if you dig down . . .'

'. . . There are remains. There are the hundred generations that came before us and the thousand generations that came before them. There is the endowment of centuries of death. That's your error, of course. Assuming that you have to make a place. It is already a place. It has been a place for a *very long time*.'

There had been a moment, in the heady scent of the squalid little office, where Napier had felt unnerved, but now he was exultant. 'Maybe others make that mistake, but not us. This is exactly what we want. If there was some way of expressing this, it could give the building . . . something really special. Do you know the Bloomberg 57 offices in the City? Designed by Norman Foster – fabulous building, and it has the London Mithraeum, exactly as you say . . .'

'Relics,' Jen said with scorn. 'The deeds there are forgotten. Deeds – a pregnant word, don't you think? Reminding us that to possess the land is an act, a verb, a continuing . . . rite.'

'Right,' Napier said, feeling that the conversation had slipped away from him a little. 'So what do you suggest? Maybe a historical exhibit in the gallery space . . . ?'

'Have you heard of a witch bottle?' Jen asked, and seeing Napier shake his head she continued. 'They're a charmed object, a ward against evil. A few auspicious items in a bottle, buried on the site. A little offering to Synnove, whoever she was, and we'll see what she has to say about your building.'

It had the merit of sounding inexpensive. And Napier found himself beguiled at giving placemaking a ritual dimension – at last, here was something more substantial than artists and authors putting in their second-best work.

◊

Little more need be said. Jen laid down parameters: sunset, on a relatively undisturbed part of the site, with only Napier, Horton, and an obliging but sceptical representative from the main contractor in attendance. They gathered in a recess that had been a basement of Synnove House, where the concrete floor slab had been torn up and only foundations and London's ancient dirt remained. The contractor used a mini-digger to make a hole, two feet deep, at a point indicated by Jen.

The bottle was Tudor, found on the site. Jen refused to be exact about what it contained: hair clippings from Napier and Horton, a rusty nail, a yew twig, 'a little something of mine'. She placed the murky glass object at the bottom of the hole, then tipped fuel from a disposable barbecue over it, and lit it.

As flames licked over the engineered coals, they stood in silence a little distance from the hole and watched and waited.

'Is there anything we should do?' Napier asked.

'Sing "Amazing Grace" or something?' Horton suggested, a little unkindly.

'We need not do anything,' Jen said, a faint odour of lighter fluid clinging to her. The sun had disappeared below the roofs of Farringdon, leaving a purple sky. Cool city air licked at the flames and the coals glowed. A siren wailed on the main road.

'I feel like I'm burying my gerbil in the back garden,' Horton said.

'This was your idea,' Napier said, annoyed at the author's flippancy. Horton, who was still going to get his two grand for a story, could at least treat the occasion with some solemnity. But why should he? To him it was all just fodder, and Napier belatedly recognised the trickster impulse of the artist. He had been made a fool.

'To hell with this,' Napier said. 'This was a mistake.' He grabbed a shovel from the contractor and strode towards the hole.

Later, the Army specialists who examined the site concluded that the Luftwaffe incendiary bomb was probably only a couple of inches beneath the bottom of the hole. Any deeper, and the heat of the fire would not have reached it. Any shallower and its combustion might have killed or seriously injured them all. Napier had been extremely unlucky, except in one respect: he would have felt nothing. The ancient magnesium and thermite ignited in a column of blinding flame, swallowing him with a roar. All around, the exposed walls of the neighbouring buildings were lit as if by the midday sun.

A tragedy, but everyone at Harbinger Commercial agreed that Napier would have wanted the development to continue. And he would have been delighted with the small memorial garden that was established in his memory in the courtyard of the completed building, between the gallery space and a branch of Wasabi. Just a couple of benches and an ornamental yew – a peaceful and special place.

A Report to the Imperial Customs Office

I KNOW THAT you do not believe me, and that you suspect me and my men of theft, or murder, or worse, and that is why you have confined me here. But when the River Navy patrol returns from Miedenthal, they will confirm my words. Not a pennyweight of silver is out of place, and they might find murder, but it will be far more atrocious than anything within the abilities of five simple rivermen.

Knowing our innocence, I have no hesitation in giving you this full account of our movements, what we found, and what we did. I will omit nothing. I only ask that you heed this warning: the silver in the customs-master's strongroom must be taken to the mine – returned to the mine – and taken as deep as your men dare venture. Once they have done this, the mine must be collapsed, and sealed, and miners must never return there.

Will you listen? Of course not. You will hear only your greed, just as they did in Miedenthal. Your greed will whisper what you want to hear, and you will follow it, not my warning. But at least my conscience will be clear, even if my memory is not.

We set forth from Kronenstadt on the eighth day of March, with a cargo of linen and tools. The river ice had eased and troubled us little at the centre of the flow, so we made excellent progress, arriving at Wollenwitz on the twelfth day. Our dealings there are recorded by your office – we sold the linen on unloading. We would have sold the tools as well were it not for intriguing intelligence provided by the dockmaster: they had heard from Hulstbruck that morning that the ice had eased early on the Mieden and might be clear all the way to Miedenthal. If we made haste, we had a chance of being the first boat to reach the town this spring. You well know the value of that: a whole winter's worth of silver sitting on the dock at Miedenthal, and empty larders and worn-out tools in the town. We'd get excellent prices there, and a shipment of silver to bring back to Kronenstadt under an Imperial Customs contract. There was a roll of the dice involved, but none of the men disputed the plan. Their eyes gleamed when we talked it over. They could feel their shares in their pockets already. Greed, you see, gentlemen.

With the money from the linen, we bought all the tools and fresh food the boat could carry and set forth again upriver. Here at Hulstbruck, the dockmaster confirmed what his counterpart at Wollenwitz had said: the ice was breaking up and the flow of the Mieden suggested it might be clear all the way. We grew in confidence. The dockmaster did offer one word of caution, which I barely heeded at the time. Now I remember the discussion, it looms larger. He said it was curious that no boats had come downriver from the town. But nothing would have changed our minds. My only thought was that this meant a larger shipment of silver, maybe even the imperial maximum.

It was a kind of lust, and having seen where that lust can lead, it sickens me.

As we went upriver, the quiet of the pine forest settled around us. Quiet, I say, but not silence: the spring spoke to us constantly in the rustle of snow slipping from branches, sometimes making ghostly bursts of white motion as it fell. Drift ice was an occasional nuisance. The lack of down-river boats was mentioned by the men, but they seldom discussed it long, as if doing so would invite misfortune. They raised the subject of epidemics, and I promised that we would not be careless if there were signs of disease. One did hear of such terrors: entire isolated villages wiped out by plague in the dead of winter. But it was rare, and they were tiny places, not a town the size of Miedenthal.

Nevertheless, as we approached our goal, the men became taciturn and went about their duties without cheer, every one of them nursing a private speculation he dared not share. The forest grew thicker and its green became blacker, and as the river narrowed its shadow fell across us. Our first sight of Miedenthal only confirmed our hidden fears. No smoke rose from its chimneys. No comforting sounds of industry greeted us. Snow was piled thick and undisturbed on the wharf and on the gunwales of the boats tied up around it. As we drew up, no one answered our calls or came out to catch our lines. It was not the glad reception we had pictured when we left Hulstbruck. The men tied us up, but we then withdrew to the cabin for conference.

'It must be sickness,' Kircher said, and a couple of the others nodded their agreement.

That had been my first guess as well, but I did not agree with the implication: that we should leave at once.

'They have left no warning sign,' I said.

'Maybe they didn't have time,' Kircher said. 'Sickness overcame them too fast.'

'A whole town?' I said. 'Two thousand souls live here.'

'Maybe we've not seen the sign,' Kircher said. 'We've hardly been ashore.'

'Then we should investigate,' I said. 'At least as far as the custom-master's office. If there's a warning posted anywhere, it'll be there.'

The men regarded me coldly.

'Any sight of a warning, any sight of sickness, we leave,' I said, with my hand on my heart. 'Though it'll mean returning to Hulstbruck with not one stick of cargo bought or sold – a tough bit of gristle for us all to swallow. But we'll leave.'

That decided them. I set out with Latham, the purser, and Kircher.

◊

The customs office was the only stone building near the docks, but it was not grand. The only windows were at the front – the rest was a plain, buttressed hulk, as befitted the storage of treasure. Our knocking at the iron-banded door went unanswered. We looked in through the windows – the shutters had not been closed – but nothing stirred within.

'There's no tracks,' Kircher observed. 'When did it last snow? Not for days. But no one has been out.'

We looked around. I saw the prints of a fox or a cat, but Kircher was right. And the snow had lain on the ground long enough to develop a crust of ice, and to shrink away from fence posts as it thawed.

'Whatever has happened here,' Kircher said, 'it is terrible indeed. We must go.'

Why didn't I listen to him? Perhaps because deep within me I knew he was right, and once I conceded, we would be away before nightfall. I could not face that loss on my books. So I did not try to argue or reason with him. Instead, I tried the handle of the customs office door, and it opened.

'We have a duty to investigate,' I said, 'so we can give a useful report when we return.'

You will accuse me of dishonest intent, entering an imperial customs office in this manner. I swear to you, we did not sneak in as thieves. We announced ourselves loudly and often. By now I was desperate for any voice to answer. I hated to hear our shouts echo out to nothing. If the building had been packed with lively and suspicious guards, I would have been delighted.

There were no signs of plague or calamity. The desks of the clerks looked as if they had all stepped out for lunch together. A fire in the grate had been left to burn down to soft ashes, and ink had dried in the wells. The air was almost as cold as it had been outside – the room had not been heated in many days. Apart from the desertion of the place, the one curiosity was the evidence of recent feverish activity. The four desks of the clerks were heaped with dockets and receipts. A basket by the fire was over-flowing with balled-up paper and worn-out pens. The side tables were also covered in paper. I had been in that office before, and I remember it being tidy.

Latham knows his paperwork and he looked over this evidence with interest.

'Look at this, captain,' he said, taking a slip from the top of a pile and showing me. 'It's the customs half of a silver receipt. Seven ounces and two-sevenths. A big slice of cheese for the miner. Look how hasty it is. The clerk that wrote this was rushing. You'd expect him to take more care over something worth hundreds of shillings. And there are scores like that.'

He returned the paper to the pile from which it had been taken and riffled through the rest with his thumb. 'Lots like that. All this should be under lock and key. It's worth thousands to the empire and to the workers here. And the most recent work is all in a single hand. No wonder he was rushing. What happened to the other clerks?'

Kircher had found another paper of interest, one that didn't need an expert eye to understand. Five words written on the back of a docket, in stark capital letters: NEVER ANY END TO IT.

'If sickness got the clerks,' I said, 'it didn't stop the miners.'

I was trying to deter Kircher from thoughts of leaving, but my efforts were redundant.

'Maybe it wasn't sickness,' he said. 'Or – not a sickness of the body, anyway.'

We ignored the counting-house where the raw silver was weighed and smelted, as it was closed off behind doors of iron bars. Instead, we went to the private study of the customs-master. This too should have been locked, but we

saw that its door was ajar. In this comfortable wood-pan-
elled room, there were more signs of the same mania that
had overcome the clerks. At the side of the room was an
iron chest, with hasps for padlocks. I have seen similar
in the office of every customs-master, and they are kept
tightly sealed. But this chest had been left open, and for a
good reason: it could not be closed, as it overflowed with
bundles of papers, bound in purple ribbon.

On the large desk beside the dead fireplace there was
the customs-master's leather-bound register, as big as a
child's tombstone. Latham went straight to it and opened
it with a heavy thud.

'More haste,' he said. 'See, captain: August last year,
and his hand is as neat as a young lady. And by December
he is writing in a frenzy. It's hard to make out the words.'

I joined Latham behind the desk. The register was
large enough for both to see without crowding over it.
The right-hand pages gave the raw numbers of cargo and
shillings, and the left carried observations, notes on the
weather and river conditions, and any other intelligence
of potential value to the empire. Turning back to late July
in the preceding year, I found our last visit to Miedenthal.
The cargo of tools and sackcloth we had sold was noted,
and the small consignment of silver we had taken back:
thirty ounces, which spent the voyage safely locked in my
cabin, and which can be found in your records here in
Kronenstadt, not a pennyweight out of place. Besides that,
the only note was: *One mast, five men.*

Latham turned several pages at once, moving into the
autumn. The pages were more densely filled, but the hand
was still neat. This period is often busy in settlements cut

off during the winter, as they build up supplies. The outgoing consignments of silver were larger, up to the imperial maximum for a single vessel. When a vessel took the maximum, it was marked by a double horizontal line on the left-hand page. Almost every boat that left Miedenthal that autumn bore a double line, and there were more markings, exclamation points and stars, showing the customs-master's surprise or pleasure at this run of success.

Some intriguing hints came through in the customs-master's observations.

Reminded men again of the promise, & dangers of loose tongues, said one.

Captain remarked that this was second load at imp. max., said another; *ensure this boat only carries less next time or he'll talk.*

Part of a longer, largely cryptic, note from October: *Third meeting on requesting River Navy assistance before ice. Contra promises, which many hold as high as Commandments. But yields consistently exceed max shipping. Too much on market at once will depress prices. Hot tempers, no agreement, more delay.*

I could understand most of the records related to shipping. But the register also recorded the intake of silver from the mine as it was weighed and smelted into ten-ounce bars. Latham drew my attention to these figures, which I had ignored.

'They must have hit the lode to end all lodes,' he said. 'Every day there's more than the last. All from the same places as well, from the look of it.'

He indicated the customs-master's annotations next to the slowly rising deposits:

> *Promised lode*
> *!Promised lode*
> *2nd promised lode!!*

'This here's the running total, silver on hand,' Latham said. 'Just piling up in the strongroom. Fifty pounds . . . Eighty! They couldn't send it downriver fast enough. Why didn't they let on?'

'Seems like they promised someone they wouldn't,' I said. 'Maybe they didn't want a rush. A rush can ruin a place. Or they didn't want to flood the market, like it says. The answer must be here.'

Latham took another thick handful of pages and turned them together. January, it said at the top of the page, but written in such a jagged hand as to be almost illegible. There were still jumbled numbers on the right-hand page, but it was hard to imagine they accurately recorded anything. The left-hand page was like an exhibit from a lunatic asylum: a solid mass of tangled, frenzied writing. Most was too scrawled to be deciphered at a glance, but my eye was drawn by capital letters:

> *FIRM ACTION NEEDED NOW against those who still warn & haver & say we must withdraw as if the voice in the seams has not been truthful in all it says! and has led us only to riches! and has kept its promises! They will make go away, and it says THEY must go, or it will fall silent, as it did wh* [Here, a couple of lines were blotted out by agitated crosses] – *It tells the truth, it has always told the truth, THEY ARE THE LIARS AND WILL PAY*

'Captain!'

Latham and I jumped as one. So rapt had we been in our study of the maniacal scrawl, we had not noticed Kircher's return. I do not know how many times he had called to me before I heard him.

'Yes?'

'You must see this,' Kircher said.

◊

He led me through to the strongroom in the windowless rear of the building. Its iron door was open. On the floor of the guardroom that preceded the strongroom, a few ten-ounce bars of silver were scattered.

I gave Kircher a suspicious glance.

'That's how I found it,' he said at once, holding up his hands. 'The door was open, the key was in the lock. It's as if they didn't care any more.'

'I've never known imperial customs officers to be that careless,' I said. 'Even the crooked ones.' (Forgive me for including this latter remark, but I want to omit nothing in this delicate part of my report.)

Kircher shrugged, stepping carefully around the precious bars on the floor, and bade me look in the strongroom.

A look would have to suffice. Even if the door was open, I could not enter the strongroom. It was full of silver. The caged racks along the side walls, which usually store the silver ingots, were packed solid – all the way back, I assume, but I could not see, because the floor space between the racks was fully bricked up with silver to a height of seven foot or so. Perhaps this ad hoc stacking of ingots had started at the rear of the room in an orderly fashion, but near the door it resembled the mayhem created by children with the world's most costly toys: a great haphazard mound of silver bars, which was spilling out into the guardroom.

I let out a long, low whistle.

'Tons, I reckon,' Kircher said. 'Tons.'

'There must be whole countries with less in their treasury,' I said. 'A king's ransom? An emperor's, and then some.'

Kircher stood with his thumbs in his belt, words deserting him. He toed at one of the bars on the floor, as if expecting it to be a trick of the light. It was solid, and heavy.

'Great God in heaven,' said Latham from the doorway. He had followed us. We looked at him, he looked at us, and we all shared a singular moment of time together.

'They've just . . . left it,' Kircher said.

'Their book-keeping was pretty chaotic,' Latham said. 'We all saw. No one knows how much is here.'

'How long before another boat gets here?' I said. 'Tomorrow? The day after? Won't be longer than that.'

I swore to you I would omit nothing, so I will tell you this: we all had the same thought. Every man on my boat could have taken enough to ensure that he never had to work another day, and the empire could not have proved the theft. This is, in fact, exactly what you believe has happened, which is why my men and I are confined. No man could have looked at that unguarded, uncounted fortune and not had the same thought.

What happened, instead, was another thought – and just as with the thought of robbery, it was shared by us all; we could see it in the eyes of our comrades. I hope that exactly the same thought has come to the men of the Navy patrol.

We didn't want to touch that fucking silver.

The quantity of riches, their abandonment, the evidence of madness, the deathly silence of the town – all of it was connected, and a terrible foulness could be scented in that strongroom. We didn't put a gloved finger on a single bar.

Instead, we shuffled out of the guardroom and back into the main office. We were as pale and hushed as men who have just witnessed a deadly accident. Through the window I could see the wharf, and my boat, and Plesser and Gutenich on deck, their tasks finished, waiting for us to return.

'What became of them?' Kircher asked.

'You hear about foresters and shepherds stranded in cabins by blizzards, losing their minds,' I said. 'Killing each other, or starving when there's still food, or stripping off and going out into the white . . .'

'That's men alone, or in twos and threes,' Latham said, shaking his head. 'A whole town? They had supplies, ample supplies. This wasn't their first winter. Could it have been mass hysteria? A shared delusion . . .'

'A very profitable shared delusion,' I said. 'The mine indulged them and spewed forth silver all winter. Maybe it was a rush: a rich seam, and they all lost their heads.'

'They lost the rest of themselves as well,' Kircher said. 'Because they aren't here.'

'The ledger might have the answer,' Latham said. 'Let's go, take it with us, and raise the alarm at Hulstbruck. Turn back any other boats on the way.'

'I don't want to take anything from here on my boat,' I said. 'And it's Customs Office property. We oughtn't move it.'

At this time, all thoughts of theft or smuggling had left me. Instead, I was troubled by something much more unwelcome and stubborn: a sense of duty. I sighed and rubbed my face with both hands.

'We owe it to the townsfolk here to find out more,' I said. 'Maybe they're alive somewhere and need help. Trapped, or captive, or sick, or starving. Who knows. It doesn't sit right with me to leave before we know. But I promise you this, by nightfall we'll be headed downriver.'

◊

I left Plesser watching the boat and told Latham to study the ledger to see what could be learned. Kircher, Gutenich and I went into the town. We armed ourselves – Gutenich with a boat hook, and Kircher and I with shortswords that we found on a rack in the guardroom. The street from the docks to the centre of the settlement was wide enough to hold a market, and with its coating of undisturbed snow, it felt wider and lonelier. As we first set out, we announced ourselves with shouts, which provoked a chorus of crows in the forest beyond the houses. Any animal life was a comfort, so I did not mind the birds. Besides them, all we heard back was the echo of our voices, so we stopped shouting before long, knowing it was fruitless.

Most of the houses we passed were closed and shuttered, but we were able to peer into a couple of windows. Always it was the same result: nothing obviously amiss, but no people. The front door of one house stood half open, and Kircher went to search inside. When he came out, his silent shake of the head told us everything we needed to know.

Once we reached the town square, we saw the first of the real horror that had befallen Miedenthal. Outside the church was a broken heap. Its contents were disguised by the snow, but a naked limb protruded, clawing at the air. We made our way over to it with grim haste and found the arm was carved, painted wood. It was a statue of our Lord on the cross, taken from the church and dumped outside like rubbish. With it was other furnishings from the church: effigies of saints, priests' vestments, wooden panels bearing the Commandments and the Stations of the Cross, altar cloths. This iconoclasm gave us pause, but worse awaited. Inside the church was the scent of death, mercifully suppressed by the cold. No longer was it a house of God. Only the stained-glass windows had been spared – the rest of the devotional works of art had been torn out or whitewashed over. Some of its benches had been roughly pushed aside, making it feel emptier than it should, and others had been broken up. In the chancel was an odd collection of articles, which at first might have been taken for objects of worship. Every one of the church's tall candle-stands, some brass, some carved wood, had been gathered there; and on every one was a severed head.

Twenty-two heads in total – and as we drew closer to them, we saw a headless body as well, that of the priest, left slumped in the raised pulpit in a monstrous act of impiety. All had been dead for a while. Since January, would be my guess.

On the floor of the transept, near where the altar should

have been, there were a number of pick-axes, saws and shovels; tools from the mine. All were in poor condition, worn down and bent by their toil under the ground. From the condition of the flagstones between this assemblage and the severed heads, these were the instruments of murder.

'We know what happened, then,' Gutenich said angrily. 'Rebellion. But why? This was a rich place, and growing richer.'

'Judas only wanted thirty pieces of silver,' Kircher said.

'So they rebelled, and what then?' I asked. 'Where did they go?'

'Fled into the forest?' Gutenich suggested. 'If the empire had discovered their crimes . . .'

'The trackless forest? In winter? Going where?' I said. 'They had privacy, and time, to invent any story they wanted. But they left their atrocities in plain sight and disappeared. It makes no sense.'

My description of the profaned church is not complete. Transfixed by the discovery of murder and blasphemy, I ignored part of the scene in the chancel. Four benches had been raised up on their ends, to stand vertical like sign-boards. The lower legs which now served to prop up these standing boards had been weighted with sandbags to stop them falling over. At first I thought this was a crude and ineffective attempt to screen off the sight of the gruesome heads in the chancel. But as I studied the scene, I saw that words and pictures had been carved into the surface of the seats. After the heretic miners had torn out the trappings of the religion they rejected, they had created some art for their new beliefs.

Stood upright, the benches made a pictorial surface that

was narrow, but tall – or deep. This was well suited to the story they told, when the four were viewed in sequence. The carvings were not sophisticated, but they had been made by someone with some understanding of what they were doing, most likely a carpenter, and they had a simple eloquence.

The first panel showed miners, identified by helmets and picks, in a shaft. Two were bent over, their heads to the ground – listening, or bowing. Two standing figures were also present, one holding up a finger to his mouth, bidding the other to be quiet. THE WHISPERS IN THE SEAMS read a title in capitals at the top; at the bottom of the panel were words in lower case, so simple and placed so low down I almost missed them: 'listen and follow and find riches'

On the second panel, the miners had dug deeper and had uncovered a rich lode of silver, which was being hauled to the surface. THE PROMISES was the title at the top, and deep below was written: 'i will show you greater riches but you must listen well and heed my words or i will speak no more'

The third panel had the title FOOLS AND LIARS BREAK THE PROMISES. Most of the action was at the top of this panel where a small group – one of them clearly a priest in a cassock – stood in opposition to a group of miners. Although it was not quite that straightforward: the priest's group included a miner, with pick and helmet, and the other group included several who were not miners. The shaft was deserted for this confrontation but for a stricken miner, who had been crushed by falling rocks. 'the ignorant ones have caused disaster silence them and i will show you greater riches' read the text at the bottom.

WE MUST ALL WORK TOGETHER was the title of the fourth and final bench. The miners were deeper still, near the bottom of the panel, where the whispering voice resided. There were more miners than before. A couple did not have helmets. Great piles of silver were being uncovered and heaved to the surface where a miner was distributing tools to a group. This group included women and children, judging by the skirts on some figures and the small stature of others. The text written at the bottom was discontinuous and scattered:

'dig and find riches' 'there is more' 'you must dig' 'deeper' 'riches await' 'we await'

Kircher and Gutenich joined me and we studied the designs together, barely speaking. After we had taken in all that they had to say, we stood in silence. Then Kircher let out a roar of rage and pushed over the benches, one by one. The din of his fury filled the empty church.

'That last one,' Gutenich said to me. 'It said *we*. At the start it said *I*.'

'More than one voice,' I said.

'Madness,' Kircher said. 'Madness and blasphemy! Miners hear and see things, things that aren't there, everyone knows that. They hear the picks in the stone, even in their old age, long after they're too weak to mine. Their vision plays tricks, worn out by the dark. The air in mines is rotten and they have visions. Everyone knows that.'

'Do you think they wanted to be let out?' Gutenich asked me. 'The whispers, I mean. They wanted the miners to free them.'

'I don't know,' I said. 'I think they lived there, in the

deep. That was their home. Maybe they wanted something else.'

'Don't start believing in this horse shit,' Kircher said angrily, shaking his head. 'Look around you. Reasonable people don't do this. Mass hysteria, that's what Latham said. Greed, followed by blood lust. And then they invent a crazy story to cover it up.'

'Reasonable people don't do this,' I agreed, 'but it doesn't happen for no reason. At least we know where to look next. The mine.'

Kircher stared at me, aghast. Then he laughed 'You must be joking, captain.'

'That's where they are, I reckon,' I said. 'All of them. The whole town. Either they need to be saved, or they need to face justice.'

◊

As we left the church, we were greeted by Latham, who was hurrying uphill from the docks.

'Finished with the ledger?' I asked.

'I've seen enough,' he said. His face was pale. 'What happened here was worse than sickness or madness, captain.'

'Aye. We've seen the murders.'

'Murder was only the start of it, I fear,' Latham said. 'They went into the mine. All of them.'

'So we learned,' I said. 'And that's where we're going.'

The entrance to the mine workings was not far from the town. A wide rutted track ran approximately parallel to the river upstream, flanked by sentinel pines. It descended into a great natural depression in the land, bare of vegetation, scraped and pitted by excavations, marked by heaps of spoil. On one side of this large natural bowl was a wooded slope towards the river, and steep hillsides rose on its other flanks. In these hillsides were the black openings of the deep mines.

It was obvious that one opening had become the focus of the miners' activities. Besides carts and winches and heaps of broken tools, there were scores of bushels filled with what we took to be silver ore, abandoned like the meanest dirt. There was also a cluster of tents around the stone building that contained the forge. We inspected these and found them as deserted as everywhere else – but it appeared that many townsfolk had left behind their warm hearths and beds and had been sleeping here, under canvas, in the dead of winter.

At the edge of the site nearest the river, we found some bodies, perhaps forty in all. There was none of the violence and spite we had seen in the church. The cadavers were wrapped in shrouds and laid out in respectful rows. We took them to be innocent victims of the mania that had struck the settlement – deaths from of accidents or the cold or self-neglect.

The entrance to the pit was a square of pure black. The sun was behind clouds, but was near the tree-tops. Soon it would be dark.

We stood, irresolute, at the threshold of the mine. I shouted into the opening as loudly as I could and listened for an answer, or any other sign of life, like the clatter of tools. All was silent. No light from outside made it more than a foot into the mine. It was more as if the darkness spilled out.

Latham was looking at the terrible disorder near the pit entrance. 'Towards the end, they had every available pair of hands digging down there,' he said. 'That's why there was only one clerk left in the office. But they were producing too much silver to tally, or even to smelt, so the clerk went too, and the customs-master and everyone else, young and old, fit or lame.'

'And they must still be in there,' I said, thinking back on the frightful, leaden silence that had followed my cries.

'I'm not going in there,' Kircher said, brandishing his blade at us. 'Nor are you, or anyone. Captain, put an end to this. We've done all we can. Let's be away from this cursed place.'

'Aye, we're not setting foot in there,' I said with a firm nod. 'Back to the boat, and back to Hulstbruck, fast as the spring stream takes us.'

'But what about the townspeople?' Gutenich said.

Kircher stamped his foot. 'They're dead, man, all of them! We all know it!'

'No, no,' Gutenich said. 'They're all alive! Can't you hear them?'

'Gutenich!' I said harshly. 'I called for them! There was nothing! No sound! No light! No life! That mine is cold and dead!'

The riverman was shaking his head as if amused by my folly. He propped his boathook beside the mine entrance and picked up a battered shovel that lay in the snow nearby. Its grip had snapped off and its blade was bent. 'Captain, I promise you, they're alive. Just listen – I mean, it's faint, but they're down there. All of them. Apart from those that wouldn't listen. And it's not cold. It's warm.'

Never – not once – never have I struck one of my crew. On that day, in that moment, I broke that rule and swiped Gutenich across the face with the back of my hand.

'You're coming back to the boat if we have to carry you,' I said, and Kircher and Latham squared up next to me, supporting my resolve.

Unchained passion danced in Gutenich's eyes for a second, and his mouth moved, still feeling the sting of my blow. I feared he might attack me with that ruined shovel and we would have to drag him away by force.

Instead, he grinned horribly at me. 'Just like the others,' he said.

I knew at once what he was going to do. But I couldn't believe it. I couldn't comprehend why any man would do it. And that moment of hesitation was fatal. I should have seized him, pushed him to the ground, wrested the shovel from him and dragged him back to the boat. Latham and Kircher would have helped.

But doing that would have taken me closer to the mine. So I hesitated, just for the shortest time, and he acted. He turned and darted towards the mine entrance.

I lunged, but it was too late. My fingers brushed the hem of his coat, but did nothing to stop him. Missing my target, I staggered forwards, almost into the mouth of the pit, and I could hear Gutenich's laughter and panting and the scrape of his footsteps as they disappeared into the blackness. And then silence. Almost silence.

Latham and Kircher had me by the shoulders and they pulled me away. They will forever have my gratitude for that. We returned at once to our boat and set off.

You accuse us of theft! Gentlemen, we would have left

our boots behind if they had come off our feet in our haste. You think we have stolen a fortune in silver and hidden it between here and Miedenthal? When will I return for it, then? Gentlemen, if you release me, I will go downriver and you will never see me in Hulstbruck again, nor any man from my crew. All the silver – all the gold – in the world entire could not tempt me upriver from here.

That is the end of my report. Yes, I heard the whispers, and not even torture would make me reveal what they said.

The Acknowledgements

I WAS ONCE told that people in the publishing industry read the acknowledgements first. I hope that's true, as I have so many people to thank. No author works alone. The beautiful volume you hold in your hands might have my name on the cover, but a great many people made it happen, some of them giving much more of themselves than I did. Indeed at times I feel that I played a minor, subordinate, role in the making of this book – which was taking shape long before I became involved. But all biography is, I suppose, a collaboration with the dead.

The editors of *Unnerving!* magazine first asked me to write about the ghost stories of Nathaniel Cruwys (1938-2016) when the definitive three-volume collection was published in 2018. I am grateful to Sepulchre Editions for supplying me with a review copy. The author Kenneth Spurless, who had helped compile Cruwys's *The Onyx Hand and other tales of the macabre* (Fontana, 1984), kindly provided some background information about the troubled publication history of these hugely popular stories, and a few biographical details about his friend Cruwys. I am also thankful to Aaron Mendel, director of *Death at Dusk*

(1988), for a very useful email about adapting Cruwys's story 'Stepped in So Far' (1967) for the screen. Mendel was also executive producer of two of the five subsequent films featuring Cruwys's character End Grusum, paranormal investigator. Professor Parvinder Bhavsar, author of *The Short Fiction of Nathaniel Cruwys: A Critical Study*, supplied vital insights about Cruwys from a scholarly perspective.

Professor Bhavsar also alerted me to the existence of the Cruwys Research Endowment for Para-Thanatology (CREPT) in Conwy, established with the considerable proceeds from the success of *Death at Dusk* and the subsequent films. Although CREPT initially declined my requests for further information, and asked not to be mentioned in the *Unnerving!* feature, this connection began my email correspondence with Morgan Cruwys, Nathaniel's daughter.

After Kenneth Spurless's tragic death in 2021, my literary agent, Naomi Yelland, told me that he had been working on an authorised biography of Cruwys, and that the Cruwys estate had asked if I was interested in continuing that work. That led to my first meeting with the remarkable Morgan Cruwys and the start of my work as official biographer. Truly there are few more formidable forces than a child devoted to continuing the work of her father. Fiona Spurless very kindly sent me all of the papers in her late husband's possession with even the slightest connection to Cruwys, including many letters, making it clear that she did not want them returned. She also offered me some extremely sage advice, and I wish I had paid it more heed at the time.

The Cruwys estate has been unstintingly generous and

attentive in their support of the official biography, paying a liberal stipend, giving me almost unlimited access to the Cruwys's archive, and the use of Amnion House, the author's home. This maximal level of commitment reflects their remarkable ambitions for the scope of the work, and its unusual dual edition: *Nathaniel Cruwys, A Life*, for all its breadth and detail, is only an abridged version of *Nathaniel Cruwys in Life and Death*, half a million words of scholarship held in a single leather-bound volume. I am grateful to the the library and archive staff funded by the Cruwys Bequest at Bangor University, who consulted on the design of the special chamber at Amnion House that will house this unique book.

Before travelling to Wales, my reading of the Spurless-Cruwys correspondence led to me consulting two experts on neurology, both of whom insisted that their names were not used in connection with Cruwys or the work of CREPT; I also consulted occultist Jonathan de Forrest and a lady called 'Whitechapel Jen', who asked to be described as 'a freelancer'. Naomi Yelland and Toby Crenshaw at Crenshaw Worthy Leung Law worked hard to extricate me from the contract signed with the Cruwys estate, and although their efforts were fruitless I understand that they did everything they could.

My thanks to the mechanics at Sterling Motors in Caernarfon for giving my car a very thorough inspection, and a clean bill of health, at the recommendation of Fiona Spurless. I am also grateful to North Wales Police for answering my questions about the circumstances of Kenneth Spurless's death.

Thanks to Hector Rosas Menichetti, deputy director

of CREPT, for finally allowing access to those papers held by the organisation that had material relevance to the biography project, and for helping me grasp the very complex and little understood science of psychocrypto-codicology, the study of the peculiar psychic properties of large bodies of text, when those texts are properly composed and prepared. This knowledge was essential for my work fulfilling Morgan Cruwys's very specific requirements for the manuscript of *Nathaniel Cruwys in Life and Death*. It also led to me consulting, via online chat, Dr Lionel North-Jarrie, an expert in anthropodermic bibliopegy, who answered numerous urgent questions on this unusual and grisly subject. Oliver Inright, keeper of special conservation projects at CREPT, allowed me one visit to the cold storage facility in the basement of Amnion House, an unforgettable experience. When writing a posthumous biography, it is most unusual to be able to confront one's subject 'face to face', even in part.

My thanks also to George and Owain, my dogged minders during my stay at Amnion House, who were only doing their jobs, and were as kind as the circumstances permitted. On a similar note I should acknowledge the tireless efforts, and often surprisingly sympathetic attitude, of Morgan Cruwys. My work on these volumes has given me a close-up view of the driven and difficult nature of her father, and it must have been very hard to spend a whole life in the shadow of that singular obsession. But her labours have reached their moment of consummation. I hope that *Nathaniel Cruwys in Life and Death*, once it has been subject to the correct rites and is safely installed in its reading room, meets her expectations and allows her to obtain answers to some profound questions. It is the biographer's rare privilege to help living be reacquainted with the dead. I pray my own daughter is as dedicated to the memory of her father – although of course Morgan might prefer it to be otherwise.

A final profound thank you to the emergency services of North Wales, to whom will fall the unenviable job of retrieving my burned body from the wreckage of my car. I hope that you are too late on the scene to place yourselves in any danger, and I would like to reassure you that there was never any chance of saving my life.

To my wife and daughter, I can only apologise. I love you both, so very much.

Acknowledgements

'Notes on London's Housing Crisis' first appeared in An Unreliable Guide to London (Influx Press, 2016), edited by Gary Budden and Kit Caless. 'The Meat Stream' first appeared in issue 10 of Pit magazine, the 2021 'kebab special', and was commissioned and edited by Helen Graves. 'Deeds' first appeared in the September 2023 edition of The Architectural Review and was commissioned and edited by Kristina Rapacki. Moral support was provided by Sam Byers and James Smythe, and also by David Green and other participants in the British Fantasy Society's writing sprints. Borja Bilbao provided valuable input on 'A Private Square of Sky'. This collection would not have happened without the enthusiasm, kindness and attentive editing of Christopher Hamilton-Emery and Jennifer Hamilton-Emery at Salt Publishing. And as ever I would be lost without my agent, Antony Topping at Greene & Heaton.